DEFUNDED

A Finn Delaney New York City Mystery, Volume 4

robert l. bryan

Published by robert l. bryan, 2023.

DEFUNDED

First edition. July 24, 2023.

ISBN: 979-8223208648

Written by robert l. bryan.

Table of Contents

For Kevin Dooley - the inspiration for the Kevin Malone character and my dear friend. Rest in peace, brother.

INTRODUCTION: DEFUNDED

March 28th: Patrick Delaney lived his life understanding and accepting reality, whether that reality be pleasant or unpleasant. After more than sixty years on the planet he wasn't about to begin mincing his words or thoughts. The last two weeks had brought him a new reality that he had no choice but to accept – depression.

The depression was consuming him – eating him up inside. Patrick always had the ability to find the shred of beauty in an ugly landscape, but now the world was void of any magic. The sky no longer seemed limitless and the chirping of the birds were no longer music to his ears.

It was dark in his living room – not just from a practical point of view, but from his mental state. The conditions weren't dark enough, however, to avoid seeing it. No matter how many times he moved his eyes to another part of the living room, within a few seconds he was back staring at it. His thought process was akin to driving around the block over and over, faster and faster. It was pointless. He always ended up back at the starting point and Patrick's starting point was staring at the photo.

On June 30, 1986, Rookie New York City Police Officer Patrick Delaney stood proudly with his father, grandfather, and great-grandfather, representatives of four generations of the New York City Police Department. All in the photo looked proud, but the proudest posture and widest grin belonged to Patrick Delaney, resplendent in his dress uniform on his graduation day.

This wasn't the first time the photo had caused pain. When Finn's knee injury forced him off the job after only a year and a half, the picture spawned the painful reality that the Delaney NYPD tradition was over. His feelings now, however, had nothing to do with his son's knee.

Patrick Delaney was empty. He nodded and stroked his chin in recognition. Of course, he was empty. The NYPD had always been his safe harbor away from the gales and storms. For the last two weeks the emptiness was constant. He was decent at hiding it, masking it with normal human emotions, but it was everywhere. Patrick also understood that being empty was not really being empty. It's because happiness is a pleasing weight that sits on you more often than not, like how air pressure sits on you, and you just don't notice it. But when you are sad that weight drops off giving the illusion that you are weightless, or empty. But you're never really empty – just full of the wrong thing.

Depressing, anxious, sad, bitter – Patrick didn't really know or care what emotion was dominant. He knew that he didn't feel good and that the photo he couldn't avoid only fueled his sad state. After the nightmare of the past few weeks he envisioned he was looking at a family of western outlaws like the Wild Bunch or the Dalton Brothers rather that generations of a proud NYPD family.

Patrick shook his head and looked out the living room window, trying to focus on something other than that photo. The last two weeks seemed like a nightmare that was played on fast-forward. If someone had pitched this story to a movie producer, he would have been laughed out of the producer's office. This story was impossible. Yet, it happened.

In the middle of a world-wide pandemic two police shootings triggered social unrest the likes of which hadn't been seen in the United States since the height of the Viet Nam War. For years, radical leftists screamed and chanted about defunding and abolishing the police, but no one ever really took these extremists seriously. Very few people recognized, however, that some of these radicals were now in positions of political power throughout the country. In many parts of the country, including New York City, the calls to defund and abolish the police were being supported by sympathetic politicians, including mayors and governors.

The New York City Charter defines the organization, functions, and essential procedures and policies of the City government, including the establishment and maintenance of a police department.

To abolish the NYPD would require a revision to the City Charter. Charter revision commissions are temporary commissions that review the entire Charter and put any proposals for its amendment before the voters. A charter revision commission may propose a broad set of amendments that essentially "overhauls" the entire Charter, or may narrowly focus its proposals on certain areas.

Richard Hays, an extreme leftist liberal had been appointed Chairman of the Charter Revision Commission by the progressive mayor. Hays didn't consult with anyone before proposing an amendment to the City Charter that would abolish the NYPD. Whether the mayor actually wanted the NYPD abolished or whether he was just pandering to his radical constituency, he quickly endorsed the proposed amendment and fast-tracked it for a public vote. In what seemed like an insane result to rational thinking New Yorkers, the amendment passed narrowly. The margin didn't matter – the amendment passed and the NYPD was swept into the ash heap of history.

Some New Yorkers took to the streets to celebrate while many others hunkered down in their homes, fearing what life without the NYPD would be like. Patrick Delaney was not hunkering down, and he wasn't fearful for his safety. He was likely the only New Yorker who understood the irony of Richard Hays being the Chairman of the Charter Revision Commission who was responsible for originating the NYPD abolishment amendment.

For the half century before the NYPD was founded, in 1845, public safety was largely the responsibility of a singularly formidable figure, the High Constable Jacob Hays. Though Hays was ostensibly supported by a haphazard arrangement of night watchmen and daytime constables, he carried the bulk of the responsibilities on his ample shoulders.

Hay's staff of watchmen was more akin to jury duty than it was to modern civil service. Citizens were expected to take their turns at it, and their annual salaries were the roundest of numbers: zero. Wealthy men could hire substitutes, as they later would to escape the Civil War draft. A salary would have addressed some of the problems—to be unpaid is, by definition, to be unprofessional—and Hays petitioned for one in 1802. In 1812 it was granted; in 1816, it was taken away, and it was not restored until 1825.

Most of the problems Hays encountered were handled by his Night Watch. Though the responsibilities of the Night Watch were serious, the institution as whole was not. It mostly comprised moonlighting tradesmen, many of whom were dismissed for drinking or sleeping on duty. Still, the experience was likely of great value to Hays, as it provided an immersive education in crime—how it was committed, and who was committing it—and his knowledge of lawbreaking became magisterial.

By the 1830s, it became increasingly clear that policing New York was not a one-man job, especially when that man was in his sixties. Hays headed a small and scarcely visible force, well equipped for occasional, significant arrests but not for wide and consistent coverage of the city. A cholera epidemic swept through the city in 1832. There were major riots in 1834 and 1837. In 1835, the "Great Fire of New York" destroyed over 500 buildings, and recession struck with the Panic of 1837. Gangs began to coalesce by the end of the decade, typically Irish or anti-Irish, often associated with political factions for which violence was an ordinary part of electioneering. After two sensational murders—of Helen Jewett, in 1838, and Mary Rogers in 1842—public sentiment shifted sufficiently for the legislature to disband the Night Watch and the constabulary, replacing them with a full-time, salaried police department.

Hays was the central figure in New York City law enforcement the last time there was no police department, and now another Hays figured prominently in the new era of life without the NYPD.

...

Finn hopped down the stairs but stopped on the last step. He sighed and shook his head. "You have to break out of this funk, pop. I know it's tough on you, but you can't keep sitting in the dark."

"I'm fine, Finneous," Patrick chuckled. "I'm one of the lucky ones. I'm retired on a Deputy Chief's pension. Age would have forced me to retire in a couple of years anyway."

"So why are you so down?" Finn asked.

Patrick glared at his son. "I'm shocked you have to ask me that, Finneous. I've spent more than half my life with the NYPD and so did my dad, grandfather and great-grandfather. Along with you and your mom, the NYPD is my family." Patrick looked to the floor. "And now a big piece of that family is gone."

Finn walked across the living room and placed his hand on his father's shoulder. "I'm sorry, pop."

Patrick grabbed Finn's hand and squeezed. "That's Ok. You know something, Finneous?"

"What, pop?"

Patrick bit his lip. "I never thought I would say this, but I'm happy you screwed up your knee in that hockey game. You got a medical disability pension and you have your private investigation business." Patrick nodded. "You're much better off than thousands of these poor bastards that didn't have enough time on the job for a pension when they pulled the plug on the job."

Patrick's tone became more upbeat. "By the way, Finneous, how is your business? I've been so caught up in my own misery I haven't asked you in quite a while."

Finn tapped his father's shoulder again. "Oh, that's alright, pop. I know you've pre-occupied." Finn cleared his throat. "To answer your question – business sucks right now. This pandemic is killing me. All of a sudden, cheaters can't get out of the house to play and suspicious wives and husbands just don't seem too interested in checking up on their spouses." Finn walked into the kitchen and pulled a bottle of orange juice out of the refrigerator. "Don't worry about me. Business will pick up and I don't have a lot of expenses living here with you." Finn took a big gulp of the juice and returned the bottle to the refrigerator. He wiped his mouth with his hand. "I'm worried about Kevin. I haven't spoken to him in a while and he must really be hurting with the pub being closed."

Patrick's laughter peaked Finn's curiosity. "What's so funny? I didn't think Kevin being out of work was such a funny subject for you."

Patrick completed his final guffaw and took a deep breath. "Look, Finneous, I've known your buddy Kevin for as long as you have, and believe me, he's not hurting."

Finn tilted his head slightly. "What are you talking about?"

"Have you been to the pub lately?" Patrick asked.

"It's closed!" Finn snapped. "Did you forget about the pandemic?"

"That wasn't my question," Patrick corrected. "I know it's supposed to be closed, but have you actually been there?"

Finn shuffled his feet back and forth. "Well. No, I haven't actually been there," he mumbled.

"You should go there, then," Patrick grinned. "There are very few things in life I can guarantee, but here's one – If there is some scam to be run rest assured your friend Kevin is running it."

Patrick grunted at the effort it took to lift his large frame out of his easy chair. He let out an even larger grunt as he stretched his arms to the side. He rotated his shoulders several times and took a couple of quick steps in place. With his blood circulating again, he resumed addressing his son. "I don't know what the future holds, Finneous. The world has flipped - everything is upside down."

"So, what are you gonna do?" Finn asked.

"I'm not sure," Patrick shrugged. "Maybe me and your mom will move out in the country somewhere where we can be away from all this craziness."

Finn chuckled. "Are you sure mom would want to be stuck alone with you for the rest of her life?"

"Don't be a smart ass," Patrick quipped, unsuccessfully trying to hide his smile. "Anyway," he continued. "If we did pack up and leave, this house would be perfect for you and Meg."

Finn threw up his hands in the universal sign for stop. "Wait a minute, pop. Things are going great with me and Meg, but we're a long way from thinking about getting a house together."

Patrick shrugged again. "All I know is that Meg is a great girl, and you'd be a fool to let her go."

"I'm well aware of that," Finn nodded. "Just let me go at my own speed, Ok."

Patrick held up his own stop sign. "Ok, Finneous. I known when I'm overstepping my bounds. I'll say no more."

CHAPTER 1: THE SPEAKEASY

March 29th: Finn was deep in concentration. For some reason, the rhythmic tapping of his four fingers on his desktop had his total attention. He had been enjoying the activity for at least ten minutes and he had no intention of stopping anytime soon. Why should he? He walked from his Middle Village home to his office on Woodhaven Boulevard because he had nothing else to do, but now that he was in his office, he still had nothing to do except tap his fingers. He had no private investigator business to work on. The COVID-19 pandemic had seen to that. He couldn't go across the street to the Shamrock Pub to socialize with Kevin either during the quarantine.

Finn stopped tapping and gazed out the second-floor window to Woodhaven Boulevard. What did his father mean with his cryptic message about Kevin? Before Finn could consider the topic further, his train of thought was broken by the sound of the entrance door on the first-floor. Finn's spirits lifted. Could this be a potential client coming through the door? Finn's spirits returned to their low level when five minutes passed and no one appeared at his office door. He returned to finger tapping, but got through no more than ten cycles of tapping when his fingers stopped, his fingernails dug into the desk blotter and his eyes widened to the size of silver dollars.

Gladys Kowalski waddled into the office, breathing heavily through a surgical mask as she traveled across the office floor to her desk. "Whew," she gasped. "I forgot how steep these stairs are. Weren't you supposed to get me an elevator?"

Finn completely disregarded his 83-year old secretary's absurd question. He had a more relevant question of his own. "What are you doing here, Gladys?"

Gladys planted her fragile body in her desk chair and rolled her eyes. "I work here, don't I?" She shook her head. "What kind of a question is that?"

Finn waved his hand. "No, no. I mean, what are you doing here today? I told you that you didn't have to come to work during the pandemic."

"You said I didn't have to come to work," Gladys responded. "but you didn't say I couldn't come to work. So now I'm choosing to come to work. Besides, I need the money."

Finn shook his head and bit his lip. "But there's no work for you. We haven't had a client in a month."

"All the better," Gladys replied. She reached into her handbag and pulled out a paperback. "I'll keep busy," she grinned. Gladys squinted and gave off a couple of audible sniffs. "By the horrendous smell I see that the terrible Spanish chicken place downstairs is still doing business."

Finn slumped in his chair, completely deflated. In trying to be optimistic he had tried to think of aspects of his life that had been positively affected by the pandemic. At the top of his list was the fact that he did not have to deal with his elderly secretary.

"Are you trying to kill me?" Gladys snapped. "Put on your mask, mister!"

Finn tried to maintain his composure. "We are much further than six feet apart, and I intend to keep it that way," Finn replied in a measured tone.

"Well, if you sneeze, I'm gonna whack you with my cane!"

Finn slammed his hands on his desktop. His dad had done a lot for him after the knee injury forced him off the NYPD. He had arranged to get his private investigator license approved, even though Finn didn't have the required experience, and he set Finn up in the office. Finn would have been eternally grateful if his father stopped there and hadn't furnished the office with a secretary. Gladys was an old friend of the family and no matter how many times she irritated and frustrated Finn, he couldn't bring himself to get rid of her. He brought up the subject of firing Gladys several times, but his dad always changed the subject.

"Ok," Finn sang as he put on his mask. "I guess I'll be moving on."

"Where are you going?" Gladys responded. "You can't drink with that drunken friend of yours because the bar is closed."

Finn forced a smile and waved as he hit the top of the stairs. "Have a good day, Gladys."

Finn turned left on the sidewalk to begin his walk home, but he quickly stopped and made an about face. He stood still for several seconds and gazed across 65th Street toward the Shamrock Pub. Like many businesses in the city, the pub had been closed since the pandemic began. A large TEMPORARILY CLOSED sign hung above the large wood door. Finn's brain kept replaying his dad's laughter and statement that his friend Kevin would never be hurting because the bar was closed. As he kept replaying his father's words, Finn began slowly walking towards the closed pub. As he crossed 65th Street he could see another sign - this handwritten notice on the door and was very small. Finn was close enough to reach out and touch the door when he could finally read the message - OPEN FOR TAKEOUT: PLEASE KNOCK

Finn rapped on the door three times. Approximately thirty seconds later Finn could hear the sound of a bolt sliding followed by creaking as the heavy door opened a few inches.

The voice from behind the door was immediately recognizable. "Oh, it's you," Kevin said as he threw the door open wide. "Come on, get in here quick," Kevin directed before slamming the door closed and sliding the dead bolt in place.

"Well, well, if it isn't Finn Delaney. That is your name, isn't it?" Kevin asked.

"What's your problem?" Finn responded.

Kevin disregarded Finn and continued his sarcastic rant. "I'm Kevin Malone. Damn glad to meet you." Kevin hit his forehead with his right hand. "Oh, that's right. I've know you since the first grade.

Forgive me, but I forgot we were best friends. A best friend usually calls once in a while, especially during an epidemic."

"It's a pandemic," Finn corrected. "And my phone hasn't been ringing off the hook either. I never realized the burgers were so popular here that you would have a big takeout business."

"The burgers are great," Kevin shot back. "Our high-class diners will begin arriving shortly."

"Since when did you become a cook?"

"I'm not," Kevin stated. "Sergio is in the kitchen."

Finn glanced into the dining room and observed Sergio lounging with his feet up on a table.

"Sergio's asleep," Finn noted. "I guess he doesn't need a lot of preparation for the big lunch crowd."

"Don't worry yourself, Finbar, Sergio has the situation under complete control."

Finn's left eyebrow raised. "And what is your role while Sergio is cooking the takeout orders?"

Kevin smiled. "I'm like the host. I make sure the diners are comfortable while they wait for their food."

"I'm sure you do." Finn nodded as he began to understand the scam. "And if the diners want a drink while they wait for their orders."

"Like I said," Kevin reiterated. "I'm here to make the customer happy."

Finn pressed on. "How long does it take Sergio to cook up a burger?"

Kevin shook his head. "You'd be surprised. Sometimes it can take well over an hour to complete an order."

"I'm not surprised at all," Finn grinned.

Kevin smiled. "There's a big defunded party coming in here in a little while."

"What?" Finn winced.

"Yeah," Kevin nodded. "A shitload of cops - I mean ex-cops," he corrected himself. "They're coming in to toast their new unemployed status."

"That should be loads of laughs," Finn commented. "Do they still have their guns?"

"Sure," Kevin laughed. "Who's gonna take the guns from them?"

Finn shook his head. "What a world we are living in." He glanced back to his friend. "By the way, if you are expecting a crowd in here - where's your mask?"

Kevin held up his right hand toward Finn and reached under the bar with his left hand. "Don't have a baby, Finbar, it's right here." In one quick motion Kevin attached the straps of the white surgical mask around both his ears.

Finn's mouth dropped open behind his own mask. "I know I shouldn't be surprised by anything you do, but you are really going to work behind the bar like that?"

"Why not?" Kevin shrugged.

"Why not?" Finn gasped. "Because that mask is ridiculous."

"What's wrong with it?"

Finn pointed toward the two huge red lips printed on the mask. "The lips are ridiculous. And combined with your height and red hair - you look like some bizarre cartoon character."

"I think it makes me more appealing," Kevin countered as he pulled the mask off and put it under the bar. Kevin placed two shot glasses on the bar and reached behind him to the top shelf for a bottle of sambuca. Finn turned one glass over, but Kevin shrugged and filled the other glass. "How's Meg doing. I haven't seen her since this whole epidemic thing started."

Finn sighed. "Again, it's a pandemic and Meg is fine." Finn's eyes narrowed. "By the way, if you are having a big affair today, why isn't Meg hostessing?"

Kevin looked both ways and lowered his voice despite Finn being the only other person at the bar. "This affair is on the down low. Its legality is questionable."

"There's nothing questionable about it," Finn chuckled. "It's downright illegal under the New York City lockdown law." Finn shook his head. "If Pete was going to risk his liquor license by hosting this party, I would have thought he would want to have a hostess."

Kevin took a deep breath. "Pete doesn't exactly know about this."

"You really are insane." Finn shook his head. "You are in here violating all kinds of laws and the owner doesn't even know about it." Finn shrugged. "I guess the lockdown laws are the least of your worries. You're actually committing burglary."

Kevin waved a dismissive hand and poured himself another shot. "Don't be so dramatic, Finbar." He slammed the empty shot glass on the bar. "Besides," he snickered, "Who is gonna arrest me?"

"You are truly a moron," Finn declared.

The declaration was interrupted by knocking on the pub door.

"Hold that thought," Kevin said as he came out from behind the bar.

"I hope it's Pete. Then you'll really be screwed."

"What a nice thought," Kevin commented as he disappeared into the vestibule.

A few seconds later Kevin returned with the first arriving guest. - a guest already known to Finn. "Sahib!" Finn blurted. "It's great to see you."

Biju Thomas had been in Finn's police academy company, and by virtue of his Indian descent, he had good naturedly accepted his nickname of Sahib.

"It's good to see you, Finn," Biju greeted as he and Finn exchanged the new socially acceptable elbow bump. Biju threw a twenty-dollar bill on the bar. "Gimme a Bud,"

"Coming right up," Kevin responded.

Finn took a deep breath." I guess what's new is a stupid question."

Biju chuckled. "Yeah, this is crazy. Who would have ever thought that the NYPD would go away."

Finn sighed. "I understand what happened with the vote to amend the city charter, but how did they actually get rid of everyone."

Kevin put the beer bottle in front of Biju but did not touch his money. Instead, he tapped the bar with his knuckles. "This one's on me for the NYPD."

Biju held the bottle up in salute before taking a big sip and planting the bottle on the bar. He wiped his mouth and turned back to Finn. "It wasn't really a big deal for the older guys with their time in. They just had to go to the pension section and retire. Everyone else got screwed."

"Some guys could still vest, right?" Finn asked.

"True," Biju responded. "But you have to have at least five years on to vest and you don't collect a pension or get the medial benefits back until you hit your twentieth anniversary - and after waiting fifteen years, how much is a guy with five years on the job gonna get?" There was a momentary silence before Biju answered his own question. "I guess it's better than nothing - which is exactly what I got with three years on the job."

"Didn't they keep anyone?" Finn asked.

"They seem to be figuring this out as they go along," Biju replied. "But, yes, as far as I know, some cops got different jobs."

"As what?"

Biju smiled. "Community action representatives. How's that for a job title?"

"Who got those jobs?" Finn asked.

"I heard that cops that had college degrees in social work or urban studies were retained." Biju made air quotes with his finger. "I also heard they took cops who were people of color."

"You're of color," Finn commented.

Biju shrugged. "I guess being Indian is not the right color."

"Do you still have your gun?" Finn inquired.

Biju laughed. "Of course. They told us to surrender our guns at the property clerk office, but nobody is going to comply. Who's going to arrest us."

"Wait a minute," Finn interrupted. " How is there still a property clerk division?"

"Oh yeah, that right," Biju nodded. "There were some other people who kept their jobs. The property clerk division of the NYPD is now the property office of the Department of Consumer Affairs. Most of the cops and civilians who worked in the property clerk division were kept on as property specialists with Consumer Affairs." Biju took a sip of beer. "They were kept on at a much lower salary."

Biju took another sip and stroked his chin. "I forgot the point I was going to make."

"Your gun," Finn reminded.

"That's right," Biju blurted. "We were all directed to surrender our guns at a consumer affairs property office."

Finn smiled. "I guess you didn't comply."

Biju shook his head. "No one is complying. What are they gonna do? - send a community action representative after me," he laughed. "Besides, this Glock 19 is my personal property. I own it, so no one is taking it from me."

"Here, here," Kevin jumped into the conversation. "I'll drink to that," he announced as he put another free beer in front of Biju and enjoyed another shot of sambuca for himself.

"So, what are you going to do now?" Finn asked.

"I don't know," Biju smirked. "If you know of any work for a defunded ex-cop - let me know."

Within an hour the bar was two deep. In theory, everyone was waiting for a takeout food order but Finn noticed that Sergio was still sound asleep in the back of the dining room. Kevin was violating multiple laws, not to mention the fact that the owner of the pub knew nothing about this little shindig. Still, Kevin felt it was important to attempt to justify the gathering by giving everyone at the bar a number like a person would take at a bakery. Finn figured that in his buddy's simple mind he thought it believable that sixty people gathered around the square bar were all waiting for burgers that would be cooked as soon as the chef woke up. Finn shook his head and smiled. It really didn't matter. No one was going to break in and spoil the party.

Finn was more concerned about his own personal safety. Besides himself, he could see only five other people wearing masks. Kevin had put on his absurd lips for all of about five minutes before it was back under the bar. Finn extended his elbow to Biju. "I'm outta here, Sahib. Good luck to you."

Biju returned the elbow bump. "Remember what I said Finn. If you know anyone with a job, let me know."

Finn nodded and began walking for the door. He took one more look at the bar, and the assortment of denominations spread out on it. He shook his head as he remembered his father's words. His friend Kevin certainly was not hurting.

Finn took a couple of steps toward the exit, but his progress was halted by the bombastic voice from the opposite side of the bar. Finn had never seen the tall, barrel chested Black male before, but he heard Biju and some of the other drinkers refer to him as Sarge. His size and baritone voice commanded the attention of everyone at the bar, including Finn. The huge sergeant stood and raised his glass. His toast was simple and to the point.

"Brothers and sisters – here's to us and those like us!"

The cheer from the bar could be heard across Woodhaven Boulevard. As Finn pushed through the door onto the sidewalk, one simple truth was clear to him. Despite the fact that there were White, Black, Hispanic, and one Indian ex-cop drinking around the bar, at that moment there was only one color inside the Shamrock – blue!

CHAPTER 2: A GHOST APPEARS

April 8th: Finn pushed open the heavy oak door and entered the dimly lit pub. Kevin appeared around the northeast corner of the square bar, vigorously wiping the bar top down with a towel.

"I see you're not even keeping the door locked anymore." Finn remarked.

Kevin shrugged as he wiped. "No reason to. Only regulars stop by to pick up a burger."

"And to have a drink," Finn added.

"Of course," Kevin grinned.

Finn shook his head. "You are unbelievable. You have been opening the bar every day and even running parties without the owner knowing."

Kevin threw the towel on the bar and pointed his right index finger at Finn. "Listen, smart ass. You made a snide remark the other day about me operating behind Pete's back and I didn't like it."

"But you are operating behind Pete's back," Finn gushed.

"Hear me out, smart guy," Kevin began. "Pete went to Florida once they started stacking bodies in refrigerator trucks outside Elmhurst General Hospital."

"So?"

"Let me finish." Kevin cleared his throat. "Before he left, Pete gave me the keys to the place in case I ever needed to get in."

Finn and Kevin stared silently at each other before Kevin delivered the punch line. "Well, I needed to get in."

Finn settled in on a stool. "Like I said - you are unbelievable."

"I don't suppose you want to join me in a drink?" Kevin asked as he placed two shot glasses on the bar.

"Just coffee for me," Finn answered.

"Suit yourself," Kevin grunted as he removed a glass and replaced it with a coffee cup.

Finn sipped the hot brew and nodded. "No matter how many stupid things you do, you do make a fantastic cup of coffee." Finn moved his head quickly to the right to avoid the flight of the bar towel being thrown at him. "By the way," Finn continued. "When you're not running bon voyage parties for the NYPD, how many people come in here every day to pick up - burgers." Finn accentuated burgers by making air quotes with his fingers.

"Enough," Kevin replied as he retrieved the towel. He snapped the towel at the back of Finn's head as he passed him. "Why don't you mind your own business and figure out how to drum up some private eye work during this panacea."

"It's pandemic, you moron." Finn rested his head in his hands. "What's the use." Finn's frustration was interrupted when his vibrating phone lit up on the bar. Finn grabbed the device but didn't immediately answer the call. He recognized the number, but couldn't remember who it belonged to.

"Hello."

"Hi, is this Finn Delaney?"

"yes, who's calling?"

"It's Ben Rothchild. How have you been Finn?"

Finn nearly slipped off the stool. "Under the circumstances, I'm going great Ben." Finn knew that the circumstances he was alluding to would be recognized as the pandemic and the abolishment of the NYPD, but he was actually throwing in hearing from Ben Rothchild as a circumstance.

"How are you, Ben?"

"I'm Ok, I'm actually in New York City and I wanted to talk to you."

Finn breathing rate was increasing. "Sure, Ben. What do you want to talk about."

"I'd rather talk in person. Is there somewhere we can meet?"

"When?" Finn inquired.

"Are you available now?" Ben responded.

"I guess so," Finn replied.

"Great, should I come to your office?"

"Ok, I'll be there in......" Finn stopped in mid-sentence. "Don't go to my office. Meet me in the Shamrock Pub on Woodhaven Boulevard right across the street from my office."

"Aren't all the bars closed in New York City?"

"It's a long story," Finn responded. "I'm inside the pub now. How long will it take you to get here."

"I'm in Queens now," Ben said. "I should be there in about twenty minutes."

"Ok, see you in a little bit." Finn hit the red disconnect icon with his index finger and placed his iPhone back on the bar.

"What's wrong with you?" Kevin inquired. "You look like you just saw a ghost."

Finn stared down at the bar top. "I just may have seen a ghost."

Kevin stopped in his tracks. "Oh no! Don't tell me you're involved with that demon crap again. We've already been down that road and I have no intention of revisiting devils, ghouls and demons."

"Don't worry," Finn chuckled. "It's not that." Finn thought for a second before correcting himself. "On second thought, I don't know what it's about."

"Then why do you look so upset."

Finn took a deep breath and sighed. "That call was from ben Rothchild."

"Who's Ben Rothchild?"

"He's Candice Rothchild's son."

"Oh, that clears everything up," Kevin quipped. "Now tell me who the hell is Candice Rothchild?"

"She was one of my first clients - the elderly woman in Forest Hills who thought people were coming into her apartment at night. It turned out she was hearing the sounds from the subway under her building."

Kevin waved his hand and smiled. "That's right. She was the old lady you spent the night with."

"I wouldn't put it quite that way," Finn remarked, "but yes, I did stay overnight in her apartment."

Kevin poured Finn a refill of coffee. "That still doesn't explain why this Ben guy makes you so nervous."

Finn took a quick sip of coffee and continued. "Candice wanted me to continue the investigation even though I knew it was the underground subway that was causing the noises in her apartment. I called her son and explained the situation and told him I was not going to take any more of his mother's money when I knew what the source of the problem was."

Kevin helped himself to another shot of sambuca. "You should have soaked the old broad for a few hundred bucks more."

"I'm sure you would have," Finn scoffed. "But Ben was so grateful to me that he began recommending clients to me."

"Like who?" Kevin asked.

"Two of my big cases came from Ben's referrals. Susan Garland, the mother of the missing girl - Chelsea was a Ben referral." A big grin appeared on Finn's face. "Brace yourself, my friend. Nancy Mills was also a Ben referral, so he was the source of that entire demon case."

Now it was Kevin's turn to lose color in his face. "Oh my God! And you're going to meet with that guy - here!" Kevin grabbed for the bottle of sambuca. "Please, Finn. I can't go through that demon crap again!"

"Don't worry," Finn laughed. "Ben just referred Nancy to me. he had nothing to do with the demons, so I'm sure he doesn't want to talk about ghouls." Finn took a quick sip of coffee. "Or at least I hope he doesn't have demons on his mind."

"Just wonderful," Kevin groaned as he retreated to the opposite side of the bar.

...

Ben looked fitter than Finn remembered. Hid face told of a lean body behind his casual garb, and his expression was serious, but not unkind. His salt and pepper hair was consistent with his 55-years, but his skin still maintained a youthful appearance.

Ben fingered the straw in his drink. "It's my mother, again."

Finn sat up straight. "She's not hearing noises in her apartment again, is she?"

Ben waved his right hand back and forth. "No, no, nothing like that. As a matter of fact, she doesn't live in that building anymore."

"Really," Finn's eyebrows shot up. "Where did she go?"

"Not far," Ben replied. "Just five minutes away in Forest Hills Gardens."

Finn nodded. "that's a really nice area."

"Maybe a little too nice," Ben groaned. "The house she bought was very expensive."

"I'm missing something," Finn interjected. "Your mom lived in a very nice building very close to Forest Hills Gardens. Why did she want to move?"

Ben shook his head. "It was all the craziness going on. The pandemic was bad enough, but when you added in the protests and the demise of the NYPD - she just got very scared."

"I'm still missing the point," Finn remarked. "How does moving to Forest Hills Gardens offer her more security?"

Ben snickered. "I guess you haven't seen any of the news stories."

"What stories?"

"Forest Hills Gardens is a unique area inside New York City."

"What's so unique about it," Finn asked.

"The streets are all private," Ben responded. "The City doesn't own them or maintain them."

"Then who owns and maintains the streets?"

"The FHGHA."

"Who?"

Ben chuckled. "The Forest Hills Gardens Homeowners Association - I know it's a mouthful." Ben took a sip of his soda through the straw. "In essence, they are like a private gated community without the walls and gates - but that is about to change."

"What do you mean?" Finn asked.

Ben leaned back and stretched his arms to the side. "I guess I should start from the beginning. After everything that's happened with mom I've become something of an expert on the topic of Forest Hills Gardens." Ben took a deep breath and continued. "You've lived around here your whole life, Finn." Ben waved one arm in a sweeping motion. "All around us is the Queens you know, with all the amenities and hubbub of contemporary city life. But inside Forest Hills Gardens is another world. It's actually a disorienting transition, like stepping into a blurred fantasy of the past."

Finn nodded. "It is beautiful in there."

"You're not kidding, Ben agreed. "It's a 175-acre community of more than 800 houses and 11 apartment buildings, churches, parks and storefronts."

"How long has the community existed?" Finn asked.

"It all began in 1909 when the Russell Sage Foundation commissioned the architect Grosvenor Atterbury and the landscape architect Frederick Law Olmsted Jr. to plan a new town on a plot in Queens. They looked for inspiration to the new British "garden cities," nostalgic experiments in urban planning intended to be self-sufficient enclaves for working people — even if they did not embrace the egalitarian ideal. FHGHA is the record owner of the approximately seven miles of streets located within Forest Hills Gardens. It has obligated itself to the homeowners therein, who pay a maintenance charge to FHGHA, to maintain and repair the community's streets, sidewalks, curb plots, lights and sewer systems. Although FHGHA has permitted the public to traverse certain streets, namely, Ascan and Continental Avenues, the remaining streets are private and the community has the authority to close them off." Ben smiled and wagged his right index finger toward Finn. "Those are the stories I was talking about. Construction has begun to seal the community off with fences and gates."

"They can do that?" Finn queried.

"Sure," Ben replied. "As long as Continental Avenue and Ascan Avenue are left open for traffic, they can do what they want to the rest of the community."

"Are they going to put in a moat and drawbridge," Kevin quipped as he passed by carrying a rack of glasses.

Finn grit his teeth, "Why don't you mind your own business and keep to your bar duties."

"Geez," Kevin muttered as he made his return pass to retrieve more glasses. "I was just trying to be helpful."

Finn turned back to Ben. "I'm sorry, Ben, you have to excuse him, He doesn't know any better."

"That's ok," Ben chuckled.

Finn scratched his head. "Ben, I'm beginning to feel like an idiot because I still don't know how all this involves me."

Ben held up his right hand. "I'm getting to that, Finn. Just be patient with me." He took another quick sip from his straw. "As I said, mom was terrified with what has been going on in the city, so one of her friends who lives in Forest Hills Gardens told her about the fences and gates being constructed and how Forest Hills Gardens was going to be an oasis of security within a crazy, lawless City of New York."

"I take it she wants to move there," Finn guessed.

"She doesn't want to move there – she moved there," Ben snapped. "She sold her apartment and bought a house without even telling me." Ben rubbed his forehead. "And believe me, that house was expensive."

"I can imagine," Finn agreed.

"So, now mom is all moved into her new home, and I am forced to take an interest in the security of the community."

"What do you mean?" Finn asked.

Ben shrugged. "Well, they're sealing off the neighborhood from the outside world, but I know that they don't have a private security force in the community. I spoke to the president of the homeowners association, and he said that the association took a vote, and they passed a resolution to increase the homeowners annual maintenance fee in order to hire a security force." Ben smiled. "The president told me that his only problem was that he had no idea where to find an honest, ethical security company."

Finn shook his head and held his arms outstretched. "Look, Ben, I'm not trying to be funny, but I still have no idea how I fit into this equation."

Ben placed his right hand on top of Finn's left hand. "I want you to run the security at Forest Hills Gardens."

Finn pulled his hand away and nearly fell backwards off the stool. "Are you out of your mind, Ben, I run a small private investigator company. I don't know anything about operating a security guard company."

"You didn't know anything about being a private investigator, and your business turned out alright, didn't it?" Ben quipped.

"I was doing ok until this pandemic hit."

"That's a good point," Ben shot back. "Business is slow, isn't it?"

"Well," Finn fumbled for the right words. "It's not actually slow – it's non-existent."

"There you go," Ben beamed. "You have the time and the need to get involved in this new venture." Ben cleared his throat. "And I get someone I know and trust who is in charge of the safety in my mother's community."

"But I don't have a watch guard license," Finn agonized.

"I'm surprised at you, Finn," Ben sighed. "In New York State your private investigator license is like a super license. It allows you to run investigations, but you can also employ security guards."

"That's right," Finn mumbled, trying to mask his embarrassment.

"But where would I find the security officers?" Finn whined.

Ben stroked his chin. "I don't know. You know a lot of cops who just lost their jobs, don't you. I'm sure there are plenty of them looking for work."

Finn thought back to Biju asking him if he knew anyone with a job to offer.

"Actually, I do know plenty of ex-cops looking for work, but they are not going to work for minimum wage."

"I understand that," Ben concurred. "I want professionals providing security in the community – not your stereotypical minimum wage guard."

Finn shook his head. "I don't have to be an expert to see that hiring a security force of ex-cops is going to be pretty expensive. Are the residents that interested in the security of their community to pay a steep price?"

"That's what we need to find out," Ben exclaimed. "Look, Finn, just come with me and meet with the president of the homeowners association – there's no harm in that, is there?"

"I guess not," Finn whispered.

CHAPTER 3: THE OFFER

April 9th: Finn looked out the passenger window and yawned. He was staring at the Boston Market restaurant on the southeast corner of Austin Street and Continental Avenue for the third time in the last twenty minutes.

"Finally!" Ben rejoiced as he eased his Mercedes into the parking space on Austin Street.

Once Ben had loaded the Muni-meter with two-hours' worth of quarters and made sure the receipt was prominently displayed on his dashboard, the duo strolled along Austin Street and turned left on Continental Avenue. As they approached the tunnel under the Long Island Railroad station, Finn noticed a remarkable transformation. The pothole speckled asphalt street had transitioned to a red cobblestone road. He now appeared to be walking along the road of an English country village complete with Tudor-style houses with red tile roofs set along parks and winding streets. Finn turned a full 360-degrees. He had driven through this area a number of times, but he had never stopped to appreciate the scenery. He was smack in the middle of a fantasy village fitted out in mock-Tudor regalia; gables, greenery, dormer windows, eaves, arcades, wrought iron lanterns – even a sort of castle-keep. The faceted tower of the nearby apartment building sported a sort of Robin Hood cap for a roof, its feather a skinny chimney.

"It's beautiful, isn't it?" Ben exclaimed as he placed his right hand gently on Finn's back to guide him in the right direction. "George Whitman said he would meet us on the center island in the square, but it doesn't look like he is here yet."

The center island was bordered by two booths. Finn wondered if these structures performed some purpose or if they were purely ornamental.

Finn turned toward Ben. "I have to ask you something."

"Go ahead," Ben replied.

"Look around," Finn waved his arm in a sweeping motion. "There are loads of parking spaces here. Why did we just spend almost a half hour circling the block when we could have parked anywhere we wanted to in here."

Ben shook his right index finger back and forth. "Oh, no," he cautioned. "Fool me once, shame on you. Fool me twice, shame on me."

"What are you talking about?"

"Look around at the parked cars," Ben directed. "Homeowners must buy a sticker to park on neighborhood streets."

"What if a car doesn't have a sticker?" Finn asked.

"They boot your car," Ben groaned. "That's what happened to me the first time I came here to see my mother."

"Booting is extremely effective, and that's why people don't like it," Finn's head spun toward the source of the comment. "A lot of people say we've imprisoned their cars, but we feel our streets have been imprisoned. Until the booting program, I had to park four blocks from my house because of illegal parking." The tall man shook his head. "People are just too cheap to spend a few dollars to park in area garages."

"Hey, George," Ben blurted to the speechmaker.

Finn sized up the new arrival. His cowboyish gait was at odds with the Savile Row suit. There was a casualness to it that Finn felt wasn't quite right in cloth so crisp. All that was missing was the gun and ten-gallon hat. When he opened his mouth, it was with a New York accent and the hand he offered to shake, even in the midst of a pandemic, was manicured to perfection, the skin softer than a baby. His face was one of upmost confidence. Finn sensed that whatever game this man played he wasn't accustomed to losing, and that included parking on his streets. He smiled like a long-lost brother and shook Finn's hand warmly with the perfect squeeze and eye contact. Finn reluctantly reciprocated, but never would he completely trust this 65-year old man who appeared so perfect.

"I'm George Whitman," the man smiled. "And you must be Finn Delaney. It's a pleasure to meet you. Ben has spoken very highly of you."

"It's my pleasure, Mr. Whitman," Finn stammered while pulling out of the handshake as quickly as possible.

"I'm sorry, Finn," George grinned. "I suppose I should have offered an elbow tap or some other form of greeting."

"That's ok," Finn waved his hand and tried to change the subject. "I was looking at these booths while waiting for you. Are they actually used for anything?"

"It's an interesting story," George explained. "In the original plan the center island consisted of a fountain and attached smaller pools which were designed to be used to water horses. About 1916 the center island was extended and two kiosks were added which served over the years as a police booth and a taxi stand." He walked over and tapped the wall of a booth. "Now, they are just for show. They look pretty good, don't they?"

"They're excellent," Finn nodded.

George moved his head back and forth between Ben and Finn. "I thought I would meet you on the island because it would be easier than giving you directions to the Association office."

"No problem," Ben replied.

"Good, follow me."

Two minutes later George fumbled with a key ring in front of a non-descript green door located on the west side of the apartment building.

"You were smart to meet us on the island," Ben nodded, noting the shrubbery and landscaping that almost completely hid a view of the door from the sidewalk.

George labored as he pushed the door open against the tide of objects that littered the floor on the other side. Finn couldn't see most of the acoustic tile floor which was littered with cleaning supplies, holiday decorations, and file cabinets. Finn picked his way across the room on tiptoes, trying to avoid the many obstacles and noting the stark difference between this dark room and the storybook environment outside.

George grabbed a card table that had been leaning on the wall and opened it on the only area in the center of the room where it would fit. He pointed to several metal folding chairs that were leaning on the same wall. "Grab a chair, gentlemen," George directed.

Finn opened his chair and did the best he could to fit himself and the chair at the table. He groaned slightly as he slid into the chair and realized he had finally found an environment more uncomfortable than the chair in his office.

George sat directly across from Finn, his smile communicating complete comfort despite the cramped, messy condition. "So, Finn," George beamed. "You want to be part of our secession."

"Secession?" Finn questioned.

"That's right," George responded. "Call it what you want, but in essence, what we are going to do is secede from the City of New York."

"Really?" Finn didn't know what else to say.

"They've left us no other choice," George shrugged. "With the police department gone, we aren't going to wait to see what kind of half-assed plan this incompetent mayor comes up with to protect our community." The wide grin remained intact as George continued. "I don't know what you know about Forest Hills Gardens, but we are in a great position to secede because our streets are already private. We don't rely on the city for any of our services. We pay for our own infrastructure like street maintenance and snow removal. All we have to do is build fences and gates to seal us off from the rest of this insane city."

"You make it sound so simple," Finn remarked.

"It's really not that complicated," George commented. "I am an attorney and I already received a favorable legal opinion from the New York City Law Department. As long as we leave Continental Avenue and Ascan Avenue open to traffic we can close off the rest of the community – and that is exactly what we have begun to do."

Finn nodded. "I noticed the fence under construction when we drove over here."

The smile abandoned George's face for the first time. "I wish we didn't have to use chain link fencing. It doesn't really fit with the atmosphere of the community." George sighed. "But we can't afford any ornate walls because we will be spending a lot of money on your public safety operation."

"My public safety operation?" Finn squealed.

George's eyebrows raised. "That's why you're here, right?"

"Of course," Ben jumped in. "As a matter of fact, Finn has already began mobilizing for this project."

"I have?" Finn squealed again.

George leaned forward in his chair. "I'll make this short and sweet, Finn. We have one thousand households in the community and we just voted to authorize the assessment of $170 a month per household for a public safety department. That translates to approximately a $2 million security budget annually." George took a deep breath and continued. "I would like a proposed scope of work from you that spells out exactly how you would perform the security function for the community for that budget."

Finn slightly nodded while Ben provided the vocals. "No problem," he assured. "You'll have the scope in a week."

Finn's mouth dropped open, but before he could say anything, George was speaking again. "There is one other caveat, and this is the main reason we are reaching out to you. We want only ex-cops to work in our public safety department and ben tells me you have a direct pipeline to a large supply of ex-cops."

Finn shrugged. "Well, I do know some...."

Ben cut Finn off. "He'll get you as many ex-cops as you need."

George slapped his hands on the card table. "Good! I look forward to reviewing the scope of work next week."

Finn eased toward the door in an attempt to avoid another handshake. Ben was already shaking hands when George looked toward Finn. "By the way, Finn, this will be your public safety office. It's a little cluttered right now, but It will be perfect for you."

"Perfect – right," Finn mumbled as he passed through the door.

An instant after both doors of the Mercedes slammed closed, Finn's frustration boiled over. "What the hell happened back there?"

"What's the problem?" Ben snapped.

Finn clicked his seat belt. "You told me we were coming here to talk about security for the community. That guy sounded like he wants me to start next week." Finn pointed his finger at Ben. "And what was that crap you said about me already mobilizing for the job?"

Ben waited for an opening to move out of the parking space, but the traffic conditions were not the sole source of his annoyance. "What's wrong with you Finn? A two-million-dollar contract was just dumped in your lap. You didn't have to bid on it or jump through any hoops. There are probably a thousand security companies that would kill for this opportunity."

Finn shook his head. "Then let one of these other companies do the job."

Ben made a left turn on Continental Avenue. "I just don't understand you, Finn."

Finn stared straight ahead. "Look, Ben, I appreciate that you are trying to help me, but I never even worked as a security guard, no less ran a company of security guards."

"These are uncharted waters for everyone, and I'd much rather see someone I trust at the wheel as opposed to some crooked unethical security expert."

Finn stared out the window at the beautiful Tudor homes. "I don't know, Ben."

"Just sleep on it," Ben urged. "That's all I ask."

The Mercedes pulled to the curb in front of 28 Markwood Place. Before Finn could question the stop, Ben provided an explanation. "I just want to drop in quickly to see my mother."

When Finn cracked open the passenger door, Ben placed his right hand on Finn's left shoulder. "No, you wait here, Finn. I don't want to get my car booted again."

Finn sat alone in the car and sighed. He was performing his first security function in Forest Hills Gardens - watching Ben's car.

CHAPTER 4: THE CONTRACT

April 10th: Finn tossed and turned but just couldn't find the right position. A lingering haze of sleep sat somewhere at the back of his mind but was too far away to reach, floating in the pool of his memories from earlier in the day. Icy discomfort blossomed in his chest and made it difficult for him to breathe. Trying to make himself fall into slumber, Finn took as deep breaths as he could, but many just caught in his throat, like an icy wind had blown down there and managed to freeze the air solid. At that moment, Finn knew this was going to be a long night, and there would be only one cure for his insomnia – two chocolate doughnuts.

Finn's path to the kitchen was distracted by the flickering light in the living room. He squinted at the bottom of the stairs to allow his eyes to adjust to the dim light. After several seconds, he recognized what was taking place in the living room.

"What are you doing up, pop?"

"Just watching some TV," Patrick Delaney yawned. from his reclined position on the sofa.

"You can't sleep either," Finn snickered. "You want a doughnut?"

"Why not?" Patrick replied.

A minute later Finn placed two chocolate doughnuts on the coffee table in front of the sofa. "What are you watching?"

"I don't know?" Patrick shrugged. "Put on whatever channel you want."

Finn took a bite of doughnut. "I'm glad you're not engrossed in a movie," Finn remarked with a mouth full of doughnut. "I need to talk to you about something."

Patrick brought the recliner back to an upright position and grabbed the doughnut from the table. "Go ahead, Finneous. My mouth will be working on this doughnut, but I'm all ears for whatever you have to say."

Finn swallowed the last morsel of his chocolate treat and proceeded to lay out the details of the offer for him to establish a public safety department at Forest Hills Gardens. When he had communicated every detail he could remember, Finn leaned forward and cupped his hands over his mouth. "So, what do you think, pop?"

Patrick chuckled. "I think you're in way over your head."

Finn stood up and shook his head. " You're absolutely right, and that's my feeling too. I'm gonna call Ben Rothchild later today and tell him to forget the whole deal."

Patrick held up his right hand like a traffic cop signaling a vehicle to stop. "Hold on a minute, Finneous. I said you're gonna be in over your head. I never said you shouldn't do it."

Finn plopped down on the sofa. "Now I'm confused."

"There's nothing to be confused about, Finneous. This is certainly going to be an enormous challenge for you, but under the current circumstances you'd be a fool not to at least give it a shot."

"What are the exact circumstances you are referring to?" Finn asked.

Patrick rolled his eyes. "Now you're being stupid, Finneous. What circumstances could I be talking about except the state of the economy because of this pandemic." He stared at Finn with a raised eyebrow. "How's the private eye business been lately?"

"Not so hot," Finn responded.

"That's putting it mildly," Patrick mocked. "I would say your business is ice cold."

"Yeah," Finn agreed, "business is lousy - so what's your point?"

Patrick leaned forward on the sofa. "My point is that people are struggling right now and out of the blue someone drops a two-million-dollar contract in your lap, and you want to throw it away."

Finn hung his head. "You're making me feel bad, pop."

"I'll make you feel worse," Patrick shot back. "You're being totally selfish."

"What?"

"You're not thinking about how many people you could help by accepting this contract."

Finn stared at his father and tried to figure out who he could be helping. Patrick provided the answer."Do you know how may cops are out of work? You could provide jobs to some of these guys and gals. Did you ever consider that?"

"Not really," Finn shrugged. "But how many ex-cops could I really hire."

"Well," Patrick took a deep breath. "Get me a pen and a piece of paper and we'll work out the numbers."

Finn ran upstairs to his room and retrieved a pen and a sheet of paper from his printer tray. "Here you go, pop," he announced as he placed the pen and paper on the coffee table in front of his father.

"Ok," Patrick began as he grabbed the pen. "I never ran a security company before, but I managed several contracts for the NYPD over the years, so I know a little about how this works." Patrick looked at Finn. "So, Finneous, I believe you said the annual security budget for the community was going to be two million dollars - correct?"

"That's right," Finn nodded.

Patrick scribbled $2-million at the top of the paper. "And they want 24/7 security coverage, correct?"

"Correct."

Patrick stroked his chin with his left hand. "I would say for a community the size of Forest Hills Gardens you would need about five security officers for each shift."

"Sounds good to me," Finn concurred.

Patrick began writing on the paper. "So that will be fifteen shifts per day. Fifteen shifts means you have 120 hours a day - 840 hours a week, and 43,680 hours annually."

"Now what?" Finn asked.

"Now," Patrick continued, "we have to figure out what you should bid per hour for this contract."

"I don't understand," Finn sighed.

"It's really not that complicated, Finneous. You have two million dollars to spend on security officers that will work a total of 43,680 hours in the year. The next thing we have to do is figure out how much you are going to pay your security officers."

"What do you think, pop?"

Patrick shrugged. "If you want all ex-cops, I would think you would have to pay them $30 and hour."

"That will work," Finn chimed. "Without working out the math I can see that 43,680 x 30 will be way lower than $2 million."

"Just hold on, Finneous," Patrick cautioned. "Security officer salaries aren't the only thing being paid out of that $2 million. You are going to have many other expenses."

"Like what?"

Patrick yawned. "To maintain proper security at a place like Forect Hills gardens, you are probably going to have to have a mobile patrol. That means having a patrol car."

"I would have to supply a car?" Finn seemed shocked.

"Who do you think is going to supply it," Patrick snickered. "And I have more bad news for you Finneous, you'll have to have two cars in case one goes down, you'll be able to continue the mobile patrol while the car is being repaired."

"Wow," Finn scratched his head. "I never thought of all the other expenses."

"Well, you better start thinking about things like the cost of uniforms and security equipment. Are you going to offer any benefits like paid sick leave and vacation – and don't forget overtime cost."

Finn shook his head. "Is that all?"

Patrick smiled. "Don't forget about your own salary."

Finn stood again. "My head is spinning. So, what's the bottom line, pop?"

Patrick scribbled on the paper for about twenty seconds before dropping the pen on the table. He picked up the paper and cleared his throat.. "It looks to me like you should bid $45 - an hour. That will bring you in just below the $2 million budget and after officer salaries it will give you around $655,000 for your salary and back shop expenses."

"That's great," Finn exclaimed.

"Don't get so excited," Patrick cautioned. "That money has to go a long way. Frankly, if I were you I would give myself a salary of one hundred thousand, but be prepared to have expenses eat into your salary at the end of the year." Patrick handed Finn the paper. "You probably can't read my scribble but it may be helpful to you."

"You've been a great help, pop."

"My pleasure, Finneous" Patrick reclined in the sofa. "And now, if you don't mind I am going back to the television."

"Enjoy, pop," Finn said as he started up the stairs, fully confident he would have no more problems sleeping.

...

April 15th: Finn needed no distractions from his task. He had completed all his calculations and research and it was time to send the finalized scope of work along with his bid to George Whitman. Finn believed it would be less distracting to work in his office, but he hadn't counted on two sources of annoyance. First, was the new computer he had purchased approximately six months earlier. The keyboard was entirely flat, it was more like typing on a table than any previous keyboard he had used. They always had some give to the keys, like you were pressing a button. It let him know he had made contact. Now, the only feedback Finn received was the feeling of something solid and cold under the finger-tip, and he found the sensation disconcerting. Then, there was the action from the other side of the office. If Finn knew that Gladys was going to make an appearance he definitely would have stayed home, but there she was sitting at her desk engrossed in the online bingo game someone had taught her to play. The thought of Gladys playing games on her computer sounded attractive to Finn at first. She could quietly sit at her desk fully engaged in her game and not bother him. Everything about that statement turned out to be true except for the word *quietly*. Whether it was really needed or not, Gladys kept the volume on the Bingo game as high as possible. As Finn tried to put the finishing touches on the numbers of his proposed security budget, his thoughts were constantly interrupted by B-15, I-29, and the jubilant call of BINGO! Followed by a loud horn.

Finn pounded both fists on his desktop. "Can't you play that stupid game with the volume off?"

Gladys waved a dismissive hand to Finn. "Oh hush. The sounds are the best part of the game."

Finn shook his head and returned his attention to his monitor. The sound of the street door opening caused him to throw his arms in the air in frustration. Who else was coming to interrupt him.

Gladys sounded genuinely pleased to see the visitor at the office entrance. "Well, hello there, young lady. It's good to see you."

"It's good to see you too, Gladys," Meg smiled.

Finn's mood immediately changed at the sight of his girlfriend. "What are you doing here?"

"What's wrong?" Meg curled her lips. "You're not glad to see me."

Finn stood and moved out from behind his desk. "Of course, I'm glad to see you, babe. I just didn't expect you." Finn planted a warm kiss on Meg's lips.

Gladys shook her head. "I don't know what you see in him."

Meg chuckled. "Oh, he's not so bad, Gladys. I think I'll keep him."

"Better you than me, honey," Gladys sneered.

Finn opened his mouth in preparation of a cutting response to the jibe but Meg's hand falling over his mouth silenced any response.

"How's your scope of work coming?" Meg asked in an effort to change the subject.

Finn moved back behind his desk. "I just finished – despite a lot of distractions." He glared at Gladys.

Gladys was back to her bingo game but still managed to mumble "What a boob!"

"Forget about her," Meg whispered. "What else do you have to do?"

Finn took a deep breath and tapped a single key on his new keyboard. "That's it," he smiled.

"That's what?" Meg asked.

"I just emailed the scope of work and my bid to George Whitman."

"Congratulations!" Meg moved behind Finn's desk and hugged him.

"Wonderful," Gladys smirked. "He must have learned how to tie his shoes."

"Well, I guess we'll be leaving now," Finn sighed. "How about you, Gladys?"

Gladys did not look up from her game. "I'm going to put in a few more hours – I could use the cash."

Finn turned to Meg, "You see what I have to deal with."

"You're lucky to have me," Gladys snapped.

Meg grabbed Finn's hand and led him to the door. "So long, Gladys. Good seeing you again."

Gladys finally looked up from her monitor. "Good seeing you too, dear. And don't let your boyfriend take you over to that drunken buffoon running the speakeasy across the street."

Finn pulled free from Meg's grasp and made an about face. "What the hell are you talking about?"

Gladys wagged her index finger at Finn. "Don't you use profanity when talking to me mister or I'll tell your father."

Meg regained her hold on Finn's hand. "He apologizes."

Finn resisted Meg's tug. "I just want to know what she's talking about."

"I'll tell you what I'm talking about. The whole neighborhood knows that your drunken friend has been opening up that bar illegally every day so that the local boozehounds can have someplace to get drunk."

"I think you should...." Finn's statement was cut short when Meg was finally able to pull him through the door.

As Finn and Meg made their way down the stairs there was a chance for one more verbal blast from Gladys before they hit the street. "Don't let him corrupt you honey. He may seem like a sweet boy, but I've seen where he goes everyday – hanging out with that redheaded degenerate across the street."

Once on the sidewalk the couple maintained their clasped hands, but it was Finn who was now determining the direction.

"Where are we going?" Meg asked.

"Where do you think," Finn answered while using his free hand to point at the Shamrock Pub.

"Do you mean to say Gladys was right," Meg gasped. "Kevin has the place open illegally."

Finn winced as they approached the pub door. "Illegal is a very strong word. He's just providing a takeout food service, and customers are allowed to sit at the bar while they wait for their food order."

Meg put her hands on her hips. "Pete is in Florida. Does he know Kevin has opened the pub?"

Finn shrugged as he rapped on the pub door. "I don't know. Why don't you ask him?"

"Well, well, look who's here. America's favorite couple." Kevin ushered Meg and Finn into the pub and re-locked the door.

"Why are you keeping the door locked?" Meg asked.

"To keep the riff raff out," Kevin responded as he slid behind the bar.

"You're doing a great job," Meg nodded as she noted the two old drunks slumped over their drinks at opposite ends of the bar. "I suppose they're waiting for burgers."

"You guessed it, my dear." Kevin pointed at Meg and looked to Finn. "Didn't I tell you that you had a brilliant girlfriend, Finbar."

"Seriously, Kevin," Meg frowned. "Does Pete know you've got the bar open?"

Kevin recoiled and placed his hand over his heart. "Meg, we've known each other since the first grade. Would I do something underhanded like that?"

"I have known you since the first grade," Meg agreed. "And that's exactly why I'm asking you if the owner of the pub knows what you're doing."

"It's kind of a complicated story," Kevin shrugged. "Pete did give me the keys in case I had to get in here, but he didn't specifically spell out the reasons for me to come in."

"That's all I need to hear." Meg grabbed Finn's hand. "Are you coming?"

Finn was confused. "What's wrong, Meg?"

Meg took a deep breath. "I'll tell you what's wrong. I like hostessing here, and someday this place is going to reopen – and I mean really reopen – not this underhanded nonsense Kevin is pulling."

Kevin wiped an eye. "You are really hurting my sensitive feelings."

"Oh. Shut up!" Meg snapped. "You know as well as I do that if Pete finds out you've been doing this, you're history."

Kevin leaned as far across the bar as possible. "But Pete is not going to find out."

"How can you be so stupid," Meg gasped. "For all you know Pete could walk in this door five seconds from now."

Kevin held up his right index finger and stared at the clock on the wall above the vestibule. He turned back toward Meg and smiled. "See – five seconds and Pete's not here. What's the problem?"

Meg bit her lip. "The problem is that no matter how big a jerk you are I still don't want to see you get hurt."

"You see Finbar." Kevin's hand was back on his heart. "She still loves me."

"Keep it up," Meg nodded. "It's all a big joke to you, isn't it?" She grabbed Finn's hand. "Let's go, Finn."

"Later, Kev" Finn called as he was led into the vestibule.

Meg made one final turn back towards Kevin before she went through the door. "Oh, and by the way. Your big secret here is not such a big secret. Even Gladys knows what you're up to here."

Kevin waved his hand dismissively. "That demented old bat needs to mind her own business."

The door slammed closed and Kevin turned his attention to the closest drunk. "you ready for another one, Joe?"

…

April 16th: The wind had bite, but the sun was high and indiscriminate on this early-spring day. Three blocks from his home, the usual choke of cars that idle on the street while dropping off kids at school had disappeared, as had the noise that blasted from them. On the sidewalk, groups of teens who regularly paraded loudly toward Christ the King High School couldn't be heard. So much of the daily rhythm made by cars and people had stopped, and it left a quiet in Finn's neighborhood that was both reassuring and unsettling. More than two years had passed since his hockey knee injury ended his short police career, but Finn was still under doctor's orders to walk every day to build up strength in his injured knee. He really tried to walk every day, but by now he was satisfied if he got up for a morning walk four days during the week. Finn's walking location was always the same. Juniper Valley Park was a beautiful 55-acre park located just a few short blocks from his home. The park contained all types of scenery to interest a walker, including several types of trees, tennis, handball, paddleball, basketball, and bocce courts, as well as seven baseball fields. Finn never enjoyed the variety of views, however. His destination was always the same - the running track at the west end of the park. The doctor directed Finn to walk on a soft surface whenever possible. Several years earlier, the old worn out cinder track was replaced by a 400-meter all weather rubber based track - perfect for the low impact required in Finn's knee rehabilitation. As ideal as the track was for his knee, Finn hated making the tedious laps around and around the track. But the walks themselves still brought comfort, and not just from the physical benefits to his knee. In the new normal of a city in lockdown there was a certain degree of comfort in this quieter world.

During his sixth lap Finn's quiet boredom was upset by the buzz from his iPhone. Finn whipped the phone out of his pocket and checked the incoming text message. The source of the message accelerated his breathing rate far more than the prior six laps. The text was from George Whitman and it was simple and succinct. There was a delicious moment when Finn's face washed blank with confusion, like his brain cogs couldn't turn fast enough to take in the information from his wide eyes. Every muscle in his body froze before a grin crept onto his face. It soon stretched from one side to the other showing every single tooth. Finn couldn't really grasp why he was so shocked. He had no preconceived notion of what the message from George was going to be. Perhaps it was his notion of what the message was not going to be that triggered the response - Scope looks good - can you come in today to sign contract?

Five hours later Finn and Ben Rothchild repeated the walk along Continental Avenue on the way to the homeowners association office. Finn was a bit disappointed when Ben appeared terribly underdressed for such an important event. As far as Finn was concerned, the inappropriate casual appearance was Ben's problem. Finn swaggered along the avenue in all his grandeur, including a tailored black suit with a charming red tie. His chiseled jaw lifted with a proud, pleasant smile. His eyes sparkling, so much like his fathers. After all his prior reservations Finn had ultimately embraced the opportunity he was being given. He was going to be able to do a lot of good for himself and many out of work cops who were struggling to survive. Finn's chest puffed out proudly as they turned onto the walkway leading to the non-descript office door. Yes sir, he nodded. This contract signing was going to be a monumental event. Maybe he would be allowed to keep the pen as a memento.

Ben looked at Finn with a wry smile before turning and rapping on the door three times.

"It's open, come in."

Finn's feeling of triumph crashed and burned. George Whitman, attired in a blue sweat suit, breathed heavily as he moved some boxes in the right corner of the room.

George shook his head in frustration. "I know it's here somewhere – it has to be."

"What are you looking for?" Ben inquired.

George put down a box and placed his hands on his hips. "My tennis racket. I'm supposed to be at the tennis club in fifteen minutes for a match and I can't find my racket." He reached for another box. "And I was sure I left it in this office."

Finn stood silently, helpless and deflated while George continued his search.

"Thank God!" George sang as his hand emerged from behind a box, tightly grasping the racket. "I can still make it to the club on time."

George shuffled out from behind the maze of stacked boxes. He stopped in the middle of the room and placed his hand on his chin. "Oh yeah," he said while hepointed a finger at Finn. "The contract is on the table. Look it over and sign it and I'll pick it up later."

And just like that, George was gone. That was the extent of the pomp and circumstance for this contract signing ceremony. Finn slid his fine suit onto the dirty metal folding chair and picked up the pen that was lying on the table next to the contract. He examined the logo on the pen and snickered – Ace Towing. The "ceremonial" pen had been provided by the company hired by the homeowners association to boot illegally parked cars. Finn signed the contract and slapped the pen down on the table.

"Congratulations," Ben smiled while extending his hand for a socially unacceptable handshake.

Finn wondered how many times Ben was going to violate this basic pandemic rule as he reached out and accepted Ben's hand anyway.

Finn leaned back in the folding chair. "My only question now is when do I have to start actually providing the security here?"

Ben grabbed the contract and began flipping through the pages. "It says here you have to begin at midnight four weeks from today."

Finn stroked his chin and stared at the boxes stacked in the corner of the room. "Four weeks," he muttered. He turned to Ben and slightly squinted. "Now, what do I do?"

Ben shrugged. "I suppose you better begin hiring security officers."

An hour later, Finn's feet were firmly planted on top of the desk – not his desk. Since there was no sign of Gladys he decided to take full advantage of her absence to relax in the comfort of her ergonomic chair. He chuckled to himself at the thought of her response if Gladys knew his feet were on top of her desk. Finn released the top button on his dress shirt and loosened his tie. His suit jacket had already been draped over the back of the uncomfortable chair at his desk.

Finn scanned the contacts on his phone until he came to the number. "What's happening, Sahib?"

Biju Thomas seemed momentarily confused until he recognized the identity of the caller. "Oh, it's you, Finn. What's up brother?"

Finn got right to the point. "The last time we talked, Sahib, you told me to be on the lookout for anyone with work for an ex-cop."

Biju's voice assumed an air of excitement. "You know someone?"

"Yes, I do."

"Who?"

"Me!"

"What?" Biju was confused.

Finn cleared his throat. "Just hang in and listen, Sahib. It's something of a long story."

Biju listened intently for the next three minutes as Finn related every detail of the story of his contract with Forest Hills Gardens.

"So," Finn recapped. "I need security officers for my new public safety department. Interested?"

"Of course," Biju gushed. "How much is the pay?"

"Thirty bucks an hour."

"That will work," Biju responded. "What about the hours and days.?

"It's going to be a 24/7 operation," Finn explained, "so everything is open. We can talk about a schedule when you come in."

"Sure," Biju agreed. "When do you want me to come in and fill out an application?"

"Application?" Finn repeated.

"Yeah," Biju replied. "I'm sure you'll have a ton of paperwork for me to fill out."

"Paperwork – yeah, of course," Finn mumbled as he realized he had absolutely no idea what forms he would need for prospective new employees.

Biju cut into Finn's paperwork thoughts. "So, when do you want me to come in?"

"How about tomorrow morning at 11AM."

"Sounds good. I'll be there. Your office is right across the street from the pub, right?"

"Correct, right above the Spanish chicken place."

"Ok, Finn, thanks so much and I'll see you tomorrow."

"Wait a minute, Sahib," Finn blurted. "I'm hoping you can do me a favor."

"Sure," Biju responded. "What do you need?"

"I'm gonna have to hire a lot of people quickly. Reach out to anyone from the job you know who may be looking for work and tell them about my operation."

"No problem, Finn. I'll make some calls."

"Thanks, Sahib, see you tomorrow."

Finn kept his phone in his hand and returned to his contacts screen.

The voice on the other end of the line sounded annoyed at having to answer the phone. "Who is this?"

"Gladys, it's Finn."

"Oh, what do you want?"

Finn really wanted to tell her he was sitting with his feet all over her desktop, but instead, he stuck to his business at hand. "Are you coming to work tomorrow?"

"I wasn't planning to."

"Well, I really need you tomorrow, and for the foreseeable future."

"What are you rambling about?" Gladys snapped.

"I'm going to be interviewing prospective employees and dealing with a lot of forms and paperwork. I'm really gonna need your help."

"What the hell kind of employees are you hiring. You have no business coming in. Are you drunk again?"

Finn was beginning to regret the call. "Look, Gladys, I'll explain everything tomorrow, but I need you here at 10AM."

"I'll think about it," Gladys stated.

"You'll think about it?" Finn's voice had risen an octave.

"Don't get your knickers in a twist," Gladys cautioned. "I'll be there – but I expect you to buy me lunch."

"Goodbye!" Finn disconnected the call and moved his feet around every inch of the desktop.

Finn hustled back to his desk and threw his suit jacket on the back of Gladys's chair. He turned on his computer and rubbed his hands together. He needed to research the paperwork he would need for job candidates and employees. Thirty minutes later Finn sat back in the uncomfortable seat. He stared at the screen and nodded. The list displayed on his screen looked complete.

Job application

W-4 tax withholding form

I-9 Employment eligibility verification

New York State Security Guard Application

As an employer, Finn already had everything he needed. His private investigator license allowed him to employ security guards, and his father had insisted that Finn incorporate when the business was formed. Finbar Delaney Investigations Inc. was legally prepared to begin employing security personnel immediately. A more immediate concern for Finn was printing a supply of these forms in less than 24-hours, especially if Biju brought a few other applicants with him. Normally, this project would be no big deal. Finn would simply make a run to the local Staples about a mile down Woodhaven Blvd. and have the copies of the forms made. Due to the pandemic lockdown, however, Staples, and any other store where he could make copies was closed. There was only one thing Finn could do – grit his teeth and hope his small office printer held out.

The error light illuminating on the printer didn't bother Finn. In fact, he was proud of his cheap machine's valiant effort. He was able to make 50-copies of each required form before the printer could finally take no more. Finn put on his suit jacket and turned off the office light. As he walked past the printer he tapped the tired machine with his right hand and whispered, "Thank you."

CHAPTER 5: THE PARADE

April 17th: 10:30AM found Finn back in his office – alone! Finn shook his head in disgust. The one time he might actually need her, she was late again. He smiled and bit his lip. What else did he expect from Gladys.

At 10:50 Finn heard the street door open. The rapid stomping coming up the stairs ruled out the appearance of Gladys.

"Hey, Sahib, glad you could make it." Finn walked from behind his desk and offered Biju his elbow. He was especially pleased to see that Biju was dressed in business attire. Obviously, he was taking the situation seriously. Finn waved his hand toward the folding chair set up in front of his desk. "Have a seat, Sahib." Finn settled in his chair and stared at Biju for a moment. He shook his head and smiled. "When we were in the academy together, did you ever in a million years think we would be here doing this right now?"

"No way," Biju chuckled. "and I never would have thought the city would have gone this crazy."

Finn leaned forward in his chair. "Just how crazy is it?"

"Law and order has reverted back to Medieval Europe," Biju remarked.

"What?"

"That's right," Biju nodded. "Our incompetent mayor thinks the public safety will be maintained by a 21st century version of hue and cry."

Finn remembered from his college days that hue and cry was the system in place in some European cities before formal police were established. The system depended on all citizens to come to the aid of a citizen being victimized and to take the perpetrator into custody."

"If this wasn't so frightening," Finn commented, "it would be funny."

"You got that right," Biju agreed.

Finn cleared his throat and pulled his chair in. "Ok, Sahib, let's discuss the hours you want to work."

Biju held his right hand up to pause Finn's speech. "Before we get into that, there's something I need to discuss with you."

"Sure, Sahib, what's on your....." The sound of the street door prevented Finn from finishing his sentence. He hesitated until he recognized the slow pace of the thumps on the stairs. Finn leaned as far across his desk as possible and spoke in a tone just above a whisper. "That my old bat of a secretary coming up the stairs. She's late again, as usual."

Biju recoiled in his chair. "You call your elderly secretary an old bat?" He shook his head and smiled. "That's not very nice, Finn."

Finn returned the grin. "I know it's not nice, Sahib, but I'll give you about five minutes with her before you call her something worse than an old bat."

Gladys huffed and puffed into the office, making no attempt to hide her surly disposition. "What are you doing now, running a soup kitchen?"

Finn ignored the remark and maintained a forced smile on his face. "Good morning, Gladys, I'd like you to meet my friend Biju."

Gladys held onto her desk with both hands as she lowered herself into her chair. "Yeah, yeah, nice to meet you Beetlejuice."

Finn rolled his eyes. "I said Biju, not Beetlejuice."

"What's the difference," Gladys shrugged.

Biju waved his hand at Finn. "Forget it. It's no big deal. Now, what I needed to tell you Finn was...."

Gladys cut off Biju's statement. "I asked if you were running a soup kitchen here."

Finn held his hand up to Biju. "Just let me deal with this, and then I'll get back to you." He then shifted in his chair to face Gladys. "Now, what is this nonsense you're spurting about soup kitchens."

Gladys pointed to the window. "Look out the window you moron. There's a line of degenerates on the sidewalk going from the office door all the way down the block."

Finn rushed to the window. "What the hell," he exclaimed at the sight of a single file line of the sidewalk of at least fifty people. He turned to Biju. "There's a huge line of people outside the office."

"Wow," Gladys sneered. "You're as sharp as a marble."

"That's what I've been trying to tell you," Biju blurted.

"What?"

"You told me to reach out to anyone who might be looking for work, so I called a couple of people." Biju cleared his throat and continued. "Then they called a couple of people, and those people called other people – you get the idea? This thing quickly took on a life of its own."

Finn glanced at his deceased printer and the stacks of forms on top of the file cabinet. "I hope I have enough forms." He turned his attention back to Biju and smiled. "Ok, Sahib, you're hired, and because you've done such an outstanding job, I'm promoting you to sergeant."

Biju squinted and shook his head. "What are you talking about?"

"Let's face it," Finn explained. "I'm going to need at least one supervisor for this operation, and I'm going to need more help than I have processing these applicants today." Finn rolled his eyes and nodded his head toward Gladys.

Gladys pushed herself to a standing position as quickly as she was capable of. "Well," she huffed. "I'm certainly not going to stay here to be insulted by an imbecile like you."

"You're absolutely right, Gladys," Finn agreed. "I think it's a good idea that you go home. I have Biju here to help me, but thanks for coming in."

Gladys was shuffling towards the exit. "Keep your thanks to yourself. I hope you and Beetlejuice have fun."

Biju looked at Finn and grinned. "You were right. It's only been about five minutes and I can think of several names I'd like to call your secretary."

"Oh, and by the way," Gladys sneered from the doorway. "I expect to be paid for today, including money for the lunch you were supposed to buy me."

"Sure, anything you say, Gladys." Finn waved goodbye as his elderly secretary disappeared into the stairway.

Finn slapped both hands on his desktop. "Ok, Sahib, let's build a public safety department."

...

May 12th: Finn chewed on the bottom on his pen while studying the notes and figures he had scribbled all over his legal pad. He began the process weeks earlier using the various note taking software on his computer, but as time wore on he found it much easier to keep track of his preparations the old-fashioned way - with pen and paper. Finn's eyes darted between his notes and the mess in his office. Despite the boxes and stacks of papers filling every inch of the small office, he was elated. It was two days before he had to begin providing security at Forest Hills Gardens, and as hard as it was for him to believe, he had accomplished the mission - he had done it.

Finn tilted his head and sighed in recognition of the false nature of his bravado. He had quite a bit of help from Biju, who turned out to be an administrative and operational whirlwind in mobilizing the personnel and equipment necessary for the project. Finn looked over at the empty desk in the office and smiled. Even Gladys had performed a positive role when newly hired officers would come to the office to receive their required uniforms and equipment. Finn looked out the window to the two white Ford Escorts parked on Woodhaven Blvd. in front of the office. The leasing of the two vehicles had gone smoothly and he quickly had them detailed to resemble NYPD RMPs, complete with a logo that was identical to the NYPD patch except that instead of POLICE DEPARTMENT CITY OF NEW YORK providing the border, Finn's logo read FOREST HILLS GARDENS PUBLIC SAFETY. Finn sat down again at his desk, rubbed his hands together and nodded. Yes sir, everything had come together without a glitch. There had not been one bump in the road in getting ready to go to work at Forest Hills Gardens.

When the figure appeared in his office doorway, Finn instinctively recognized it was far more than a bump in the road. This was a huge pot hole in the shape of a 6foot 5-inch body with red hair.

"What's up buddy?" Kevin sang as he entered the office.

Finn noted the 11:20AM displaying on the screen of his iPhone. "What are you doing here? I thought you'd be running your illegal speakeasy."

Kevin smiled and shrugged. "All good things come to an end, right?"

Finn pushed his chair back from his desk. "What's that supposed to mean?"

"It means I'm not doing that anymore."

"Why?"

Kevin strolled to the window and stared out to the boulevard. "Well, let's just say Pete didn't fully endorse what I was doing."

Finn shook his head. "I told you this would happen. Who called him in Florida?"

"No one called him," Kevin replied.

"Then how did he find out?"

Kevin turned his head toward Finn. "Pete walked into the bar yesterday when I was serving some customers."

"And?" Finn waited for the climax, even though he knew what the end of the story would be.

Kevin shrugged. "And he fired me on the spot."

Finn wagged a finger toward Kevin. "I told you this would happen, but you never learn."

"It was worse than that," Kevin continued. "Pete said that if there were still police in the city he would have instantly had me locked up for burglary and grand larceny."

"Good for him," Finn nodded. "Why didn't he do it?"

"Pete said it was too difficult to figure out who handled this now in the city bureaucracy."

"So, he let you off the hook," Finn commented.

"Not really," Kevin responded. "He said he wants two thousand dollars from me for the booze and food I went through, and that if I don't start paying him, he will figure out the process to send me to jail, regardless of how complicated it is."

Finn took a deep breath and went back to studying his legal pad. "Well, all I can do is wish you much luck and recommend Mexico as a hiding place for you."

"Come on, Finbar," Kevin whined. "be serious. I'm in a tight spot here."

"That's right!" Finn pounded the pen onto the desktop. "You're in a tight spot - not me!"

Kevin hung his head and shuffled his feet. "Yeah, but you can help me."

Finn pounded both fists on the desk top and shot up out of his chair. "I knew it! Here it comes! You screw up again and now you concoct some hairbrained scheme that gets me involved. When does your nonsense ever end?"

There was a glazed look in Kevin's eyes as he sighed and slowly walked toward the exit. "Sorry," he mumbled.

Finn sat as his desk gritting his teeth and rhythmically tapping the desktop with his fingers as he listened to the sound of Kevin's footsteps fade. When he heard the street door open a very low "Damn it" was followed by the shout of "Kevin - get back here!"

Ten minutes later Finn sat with his head in his hands, trying not to think about the headache that was building, both literally and symbolically. "Look," he said while extending his hands towards Kevin. "Even if I wanted to I can't hire you."

"Why not?"

"Duh!" Finn mocked. "Have you forgotten the bogus security school you were running last year. You are blackballed by the Department of State and can't get a security license."

Kevin scratched his head. "Well, I don't have to be a security guard. Don't you need a secretary, or an administrative guy - even a janitor?"

Finn rose from his desk and went to the window. As much as he hated to admit it, Kevin may have had a good idea. Gladys was going to stay at the office, not because of the investigation business duties, but because she refused to relocate anywhere she couldn't walk to. Biju was going to be an operational patrol supervisor with little time to devote to administrative duties. Unless Finn wanted to handle every administrative task himself, he could use support - but this was Kevin, perhaps the most unreliable person on the planet. But this was also his lifelong friend and he knew how this story was going to end so he may as well stop fooling himself. Finn cleared his throat and tried to use a boss voice. "Ok, this is the deal. I'll hire you as my administrative assistant. Your salary will be minimum wage."

"Minimum wage?" Kevin blurted.

"That's right," Finn snapped. "I have no budget for this job so your salary is actually coming out of my salary."

"Yeah, I know," Kevin extended his arms to the side. "But minimum wage?"

It had taken all of two minutes for the sympathy to drain from Finn's body. "Look" he pointed, "There's the door. Take it or leave it."

"Alright," Kevin moaned. "Don't be so sensitive."

With his headache building and his concentration focused completely on Kevin, Finn had not heard the street door or the thumping slowly coming up the stairs. The greeting at the office door caught him completely off guard. "Well, well if it isn't tweedle dum and tweedle dee, or is that tweedle drunk."

"I didn't know you were coming in today, Gladys?" Finn remarked.

"What's wrong?" Gladys scoffed as she hobbled across the floor. "Are you keeping track of my schedule?"

A wry smile appeared on Finn's face. "Well, I am your boss."

"What an old bat," Kevin mumbled under his breath.

"I heard that!" Gladys pointed a boney finger at Kevin. "The whole neighborhood knows that Pete wants to put you in jail. I suppose you came here to find a cell mate." The finger now focused on Finn. "And this idiot is just stupid enough to let you take him down with you."

Finn rose from his chair. "Let's take a walk, Kev."

"Where to?"

"That's right," Gladys interrupted. "You can't go across the street to the bar anymore. Why don't you go over to the bench by the bus stop and drink your booze out of paper bags like a couple of real stumblebums."

Finn pushed Kevin toward the office door. "Have a good day, Gladys."

"Yeah," Kevin sneered. "It's always a pleasure."

"Ahh!, Blow it out your ass," Gladys groaned. "And don't forget to close the door."

•••

May 7th: It was T-minus one day until the official birth of the Forest Hills Public Safety Department. Finn had everything planned as if it was the grand opening of a supermarket. Even though the security coverage didn't begin until the next day, Finn had directed all his officers to assemble at Flagpole Park at 11AM. At the circular seating area of high-back benches at the head of the village green, residents could gather in the shade of chestnut trees to chat in good weather. Just beyond was Flagpole Park, dominated by the former mainmast of the yacht Columbia, America's defender of the America's Cup in 1898 and

1901. One hundred feet tall, and capped with the figure of a seagull that was often mistaken for an eagle.

At 9AM Finn put the finishing touches on a bowel of Special-K and a large glass of orange juice. He instantly recognized the number displaying on his iPhone's screen.

"Shit!" he groaned before connecting to the call. "Hello."

"Hi, Finn. This is Sheila from Dr. Larson's office. You have an appointment for 9AM. Are you on your way?

"I'm so sorry, Sheila. The appointment completely slipped my mind. Can I reschedule?"

Sheila's previous pleasant tone had disintegrated. "It's very difficult keeping the schedule during this pandemic and Dr. Larson is going on vacation next week. If you don't come in now I'm not going to be able to get you in until sometime in September."

Finn kept the phone to his right ear and massaged his forehead with his left hand. He realized the importance of having his knee checked, and it just wouldn't be smart to put off the examination for several months. "Ok, I'll be there in twenty minutes."

Immediately upon disconnecting from the doctor's office, Finn connected to a new phone number.

"What's up?" Kevin sang.

"I need you to do something for me," Finn stated.

"Your wish is my command, master."

"Will you shut up and just listen," Finn pled.

"Lay it on me, boss." Kevin replied.

"I completely forgot about my knee check up with Dr. Larson today. I have to go there now, but I still think I can make it over to Forest Hills Gardens by 11AM."

"What do you want me to do?" Kevin asked.

"Not much," Finn cautioned. "Just get to Flagpole Park at 10AM and just greet the staff as they arrive – take their names and tell them they are in the right place."

"I think I can handle that," Kevin bragged.

"That's all I want you to do," Finn warned. "Don't do anything else until I get there."

"10-4 chief," Kevin snapped. "I know you can't see me, but I'm standing at attention and saluting."

"Jerk!" Finn mumbled as he disconnected the call.

•••

Finn felt a twinge of pain in his knee as he lengthened his stride. He had not yet asked George Whitman about a parking permit, so the new director of public safety still had to park outside of Forest Hills Gardens because he did not want to risk getting his car booted. Finn noted that the commercial clutter at the intersection of Austin Street and 71st Avenue was lively but ordinary. He still found it hard to imagine that one block away was the verdant, precisely planned community of Forest Hills Gardens.

The neatly trimmed grass covering Flagpole Park was a shade of perfect deep green Finn didn't believe he had ever seen before. He scanned the area, taking a second or two to let the new information sink in, even though it was right before his eyes, larger than life. Except for an elderly couple seated on a bench and a solo elderly woman to their right performing stretching exercises, the park was empty. Where the hell were his security officers and where the hell was Kevin?

Finn could feel his face turning red with suppressed rage, his knuckles now white from clenching his fist too hard, and his teeth gritted from an effort not to scream all manner of obscenities. In the midst of his rage Finn's attention was oddly drawn to the elderly woman going through her exercise routine. It wasn't just stretching. To Finn it looked like some type of dance – almost like ballet but not quite as strenuous. Finn stared at her in awe, wondering how one so old, fragile and tiny could achieve this level of talent. She moved with feeling on that grassy stage, pouring forth an outburst of emotions through her movements, not only moving her body, but moving her soul. For the moment, Finn had completely forgotten about Kevin and his officers as he became lost in her movements. It was truly breathtaking.

Finn had fallen into something similar to a trance that was only broken by its source.

"Mr. Delaney, is that you?"

Finn suddenly recognized the subject of his admiration. "Ms. Rothchild. I didn't know that was you. It's good to see you again."

"Did you enjoy my show?" she smiled.

"It was beautiful," Finn gushed. "It looked a little like ballet."

"It should," Candice Rothchild giggled. "I danced ballet for over fifty years." She sighed deeply. "At 85 I can only go through the movements very slowly, but it still keeps my blood circulating."

"It looked wonderful," Finn praised.

Candice bowed slightly. "Well, thank you, sir. It's good to still have a fan at my age."

"Your son told me you bought a house in the community. How do you like it?"

Candice performed an artistic sweep of her arms. "It's beautiful here. I love it – especially with all the craziness in the world I feel safe here."

"That's good," Finn remarked.

Candice's face lit up. "Ben told me about you providing security for the community. I think that's great. When do you start?"

Finn shrugged. "Funny you should ask me that, Ms. Rothchild. That's the reason I'm here right now."

"Oh, really?"

"Yes, you see today we are...." Finn's voice faded when he picked up a sound far in the distance. It was a strange yet familiar sound, and it had now caught the attention of Candice Rothchild and the couple on the bench.

"What is that sound?" Candice asked.

Finn nodded in recognition. It was the unmistakable skirl of a bagpipe.

The scene was unbelievable – shocking really. Finn's mind was sent reeling, unable to process or comprehend the images being sent to his eyes. He looked away, then looked back to see if the scene was still the same – it was. With years of experience in the shenanigans of Kevin Malone, Finn did not think it was possible for his friend to do anything that could shock him. Yet, there he was, planted on the grassy expanse, in a state of complete shock.

"Oh look," Candice sang. "A parade!"

"It sure looks like a parade," Finn nodded, still in a state of disbelief. There was no more need for words as Finn and Candice took in the spectacle marching down Greenway Terrace. A lone piper played Garryowen as he strode in front of sixty uniformed public safety officers, who marched proudly in step in columns of six to the cadence provided by the pipe. Behind the parading uniformed personnel at least a hundred residents of the community had happily joined the march. The coup de gras to the bizarre scene was directly in front of the piper. Leading the entire parade down the street was Kevin Malone, strutting along like a seasoned drum major. He even appeared to be wielding a mace in his right hand. Finn rubbed his eyes. Drum Major's maces have been in existence since the 17th century, with functional uses in the British Army Regiments. Their main use was to define drill movements and signal commands to the band members. How the hell did Kevin get his hands on this ceremonial staff with an ornate head. As Kevin drew closer Finn received his answer. Kevin's mace was actually a golf club - a 3-wood to be specific.

Drum Major Malone broke away from the parade and approached Finn, still wielding his ceremonial golf club. The wide grin on his face left no mistake about it. Kevin was extremely proud of the event he had just staged.

Words had left Finn. He stared into Kevin's bright blue eyes, his own eyes burning with anger. Finn had a lot he wanted to say, but he couldn't will his lips to move. As if stuck underwater, everything was slow and warbled as he pointed a shaky finger in Kevin's face. "Do you have anything to say?"

Kevin looked at Finn, then at the assemblage of uniforms and residents in the park, and then back to Finn. Kevin's smile grew wider. "Isn't this great?" he announced.

At that moment, all the anger drained from Finn like the air being released from a balloon. What could he do? This was his buddy Kevin, and nothing he did should be a total shock.

With renewed composure, Finn still wanted the details of what he had just witnessed. "Can you please tell me what just happened here?"

"You're not gonna believe this, Finbar," Kevin gushed. "But I didn't plan this. It just came to me on the fly."

"Oh, don't worry, buddy. I believe you," Finn moaned.

"The only thing planned," Kevin clarified, "was Sean Muldoon. Sean was in the Emerald Society Pipe Band and when you told me to notify these guys to be here today, I thought it would be nice if Sean played a few tunes in the park."

"And he said yes?" Finn questioned.

"Sure," Kevin shrugged. "I know Sean – as a matter of fact I know half these guys from the bar."

Finn squinted slightly. "That still doesn't tell me how this parade started."

"So," Kevin continued. "Everyone is starting to mill around on the grass and Sean asks me if he should start playing. I told him to play, but before he starts he makes a comment that it's gonna be strange for him to play while standing still because he usually plays while marching."

Finn scratched his head. "So, you told everyone to..."

Kevin punched Finn on the right arm and cut him off in mid-sentence. "That's right, Finn, my boy. I grabbed my 3-wood out of the trunk of my car, assembled the troops, and the rest is history."

Finn shook his head. "Unbelievable!"

"They loved us!" Kevin shot back. "You should have seen them lining the streets as we marched by." He glanced at the crowd in the park. "And look how many followed us here."

"Finn! Finn!" The call was mixed with a boisterous laugh. The laugh came from George Whitman like a newly sprung leak - timid at first, stopping and starting. He wasn't done yet though. Finn could tell from the way he rolled his eyes to the sky and half bit his lip. From deep inside his chest came a great shaking motion and his face muscles grew tight. Finn folded his arms, eyebrows arched, waiting.

"Why didn't you tell me you were going to do that? That was great." That was the only statement George could manage. In an instant his laugh was more like a burst water main arching into the brilliant summer sky soaking everyone around him with unrestrained gales that debilitated him to a thigh slapping and pick faced picture of glee.

Finn wanted to stay straight faced, flip his hair and storm off. Instead, he returned the smile. "Glad you enjoyed it, George."

"Well," George continued as he attempted to catch his breath. "Go ahead."

"Go ahead?" Finn repeated as a question.

George waved his arm toward the crowd assemble on the green. "Address the community. That's why you brought them here, right?"

Finn scanned the crowd on the green and cleared his throat. "Good morning everyone," he exclaimed in a volume that attracted no one's attention.

"That's not gonna do it," Kevin grinned. "EVERYONE, LISTEN UP – NOW!" he bellowed. With all eyes turned towards them, Kevin relinquished the floor. "It's all yours, chief."

Finn took a deep breath, but no words had formed in his mouth. He was beginning to sense curious looks from the crowd and he could feel himself beginning to panic. He couldn't stand there like a boob any longer. He had to say something.

"Today, is a historic day for Forest Hills Gardens." Finn bit his lip as he tried to pull the words back. Who was he supposed to be – Winston Churchill? He knew he had to wrap up before he embarrassed himself. "We look forward to serving the community to the best of our ability. Thank you."

The smattering of polite applause convinced Finn that he had not made a complete fool of himself.

Kevin slapped Finn's back. "Great job, boss!" Finn glared at his friend, waiting for a punch line that never came.

"Finn, I need to talk to you." George Whitman's wide smile was still a fixture on his face, but he had recovered from his recent laughing fit. "I need to show you around some areas of the community."

Finn held up his right hand. "Give me two minutes, George." He wheeled around toward Kevin and handed him a file folder. "This is the schedule for the next two weeks and a roster. Make sure everyone signs the roster acknowledging that they know their schedule."

Kevin grabbed the schedule, clicked his heels together and performed an exaggerated salute. "Yes sir, general!" he cheered.

"Cut the crap." Finn grumbled as he departed with George.

"Are you in the mood for a little exercise, Finn," George proposed.

"Why not?" Finn shrugged. The twinge in his knee was saying otherwise, but no more than an hour ago Dr. Larson emphasized the importance of keeping up with his walking regimen.

It took the duo a little over an hour to stroll the 3.5 mile perimeter of the community. There was nothing exceptional about the 8-foot chain link fence, but George had plenty to say about the access points to the community. It seemed that the residents had voted that there should be two vehicle entry points – one at the north end of the community at Station Square and the other on the south side at Continental Avenue and Metropolitan Avenue. These two locations had security booths with electronic arms that Finn's officers would operate from inside the booths. George mentioned that there were several other vehicle gates along the perimeter that were required by the fire code, but that these emergency access points would be kept locked. George also pointed out the six pedestrian turnstiles spread around the perimeter. From the inside a person could push through the iron turnstile with no clearance required. From the outside, however, a proxinity card had to be tapped on a reader to allow the turnstile to turn. George mentioned that all the residents had been issued proximity cards.

When they reached Station Square Finn balked at venturing any further. "My car is parked on Austin Street, George, so I'm gonna hit the road."

"Ok, Finn," George replied. "I'll have a parking permit ready for you tomorrow."

"Sounds good, George – thanks."

George's smile was immense. "Tomorrow will be an exciting day, right?"

"It certainly will be," Finn agreed.

"By the way," George inquired. "What will your uniform look like?"

"My uniform?" Finn gasped.

"Of course," George responded. "The director of public safety will wear a uniform. It's in the scope of work – didn't you read that?"

"No problem," Finn sighed in accepting his fate. "I'll be in uniform."

"Ok then," George continued smiling and extended his hand, but quickly transitioned to an elbow tap. "See," he bragged. "I'm learning all these pandemic rules."

CHAPTER 6: THE GENERAL

My 8th: Finn gazed at his reflection in the full-length mirror. He didn't see the trim young man in the crisp light blue uniform shirt with navy blue trousers. Finn's eyes could focus on one item and one item only – the square badge. From the first day he could walk, Finn's father had preached that there was no shame in any honest work, but that square badge was a tough pill to swallow. Finn realized that there were thousands of very professional security officers working in all areas of business and industry, but "square-badge" was an all too common nickname used to belittle the occupation. And now, here he was, with a shiny square badge pinned to his shirt at his left breast.

New York State law left Finn little choice in the badge selection for his company. To reduce the chances of private security officers being mistaken for police officers, only square badges were authorized for security officers. As Finn took a final look at himself in the mirror he wondered if that law would change in New York City. After all, since there was no more NYPD, who would security officers be mistaken for? Well, at least he could hope.

Finn was running later than he wanted to so he decided to skip breakfast and head directly out the door to his car. His path to the door was interrupted by a voice from the living room.

"Wait a minute!" Patrick Delaney rose from his recliner and met Finn at the foyer. "You look sharp, Finneous."

Finn did not respond. He was unsure if his father was being sincere, or if he was making a sarcastic remark about his square badge.

Finn pointed to the door. "I have to get going, pop. I can't be late for the first day."

"Just one more second," Patrick grinned as he reached into his right pants pocket. "Under the circumstances, I think these will be perfect for you."

"What are you doing?" Finn mumbled as his father went to work. He very quickly attached a small gold star to each side of Finn's shirt collar.

Patrick took a step back and admired his work. "There you go. Those stars are the collar insignia I wore as a deputy chief on the NYPD. I have no more use for them. You're the chief in that community. You should have something to distinguish yourself, right?"

"Sure, pop. Thanks." Finn burst through the door before his father could produce something else – maybe a ceremonial hat with large feathers. Finn sighed deeply as he pulled away from the front of his house. He felt ridiculous enough wearing the square badge. Now, he couldn't wait for the reaction he would receive to his stars.

Finn glanced in the rear view mirror and smiled at the sight of the Forest Hills Gardens parking permit affixed securely to his rear windshield. The guard booth at Station Square was empty and the arms at both the entrance and exit lanes were fixed in the up position. In about 45-minutes everything was going to change.

Finn pulled to the curb adjacent to his new office. He already noticed a difference with the door. George Whitman had tasked the community maintenance man to create a sign. The result was not exactly a sign, but Finn was more than satisfied with the stenciled white paint on the door identifying the location as the PUBLIC SAFETY DEPARTMENT.

When Finn entered the office, Biju was already inside. Finn stared as if Biju just produced a rhinoceros from his pocket. He couldn't imagine it was the same office where he had signed the contract several weeks earlier. The boxes, clutter and junk were gone, replaced by two desks, a table and several file cabinets. On top of a file cabinet was a base station with charging ports for a dozen walkie talkie radios. On the table was a clipboard with the roll call for the 8AM shift.

"Sahib, you've outdone yourself," Finn gushed. "I wouldn't have known this was the same office."

"Thanks," Biju replied. "You've outdone yourself too," He grinned while pointed to the stars on Finn's collar.

"Forget about the stars," Finn grumbled. "Tell me what you've done here."

Biju spun toward the desks. "I figured one desk would be yours and the other would be for the shift supervisor."

"Sounds good," Finn nodded.

Biju switched his focus to the table. "We'll always keep the upcoming roll call on the table for the guys to sign on and off duty. This way the supervisor can check to see if anyone is AWOL."

"Good idea," Finn concurred.

Biju tapped the top of the table. "Whoever is on meal break could also use the table to eat if they wanted to."

Finn placed his hands on his hips and shook his head. "You've done an unbelievable job, Sahib. I think we're ready to roll."

Biju glanced at Finn's stars and smiled. "10-4 Chief. The radios are charged, the patrol car is gassed and the booths are waiting for bodies to occupy them. We are ready!"

Kevin entered the office, and for an instant he stood statue-like, wide eyed and silent. The silence abruptly ended when he suddenly doubled himself up and burst into a loud harsh cackle of laughter, with the side of the table the only thing preventing a flop to the floor. He was beside himself, in a sort of hysterics. He could not help himself as he struggled to blurt his message. "Where's your helmet, General Patton?" No more words were possible as laughter consumed his entire being.

…

May 15th: The honeymoon lasted exactly one week, at least for Richard and Ellen Sherman. The Sherman's had just returned from a weekend in Connecticut to find a rear window to their home jimmied open and most of Ellen's jewelry gone.

Finn stroked his chin as he stared at the damaged window. He pulled a small notebook and pen from his shirt pocket, just above his square badge. He opened the book and put the pen to the page – and stopped. Instinctively, Finn knew he should be taking notes regarding the crime scene, but he didn't really have a clue as to what he should be looking for.

Richard Sherman had been walking in small circles ranting at no one in particular. Suddenly, his internal radar locked onto a target.

"You – yeah, you with all the stars. What are you going to do about this? Why do we have you here?"

Finn maintained his composure but only made the situation worse. "Don't you have an alarm, Mr. Sherman?"

"An alarm!" Sherman waved his arms wildly. "You're supposed to be my alarm. Do you know how much I am paying each month to have you here protecting us?"

"Chief." Biju called to Finn as Sherman broke off his attack and began a renewed general rant.

"What are we supposed to do?" Finn whispered.

"Well," Biju cleared his throat and pointed to the clipboard in his hand. "Mrs. Sherman gave me the names of every contractor and delivery person she could remember coming into her home for the last month." He flipped to the next sheet of paper on the clipboard. "I also have the log book entries from the guard booths with the list of visitors for the last three days."

Finn shrugged. "Well, it's something, I guess."

"Too bad there's no cameras," Biju commented.

Finn shook his head. "The Sherman's have no cameras and Whitman told me they spent enough this year in bringing us in. Cameras may be budgeted for next year."

Finn inched closer to Biju and leaned in toward his ear. "So, now what do we do. There's no more police department so who do we call?"

"We call 311," Biju replied.

"311?" Finn scoffed. "That's for reporting issued like potholes, not burglaries."

"Your forgetting about this brave new world we live in," Biju corrected. "311 will connect us to the Mayor's Community Response Network."

"And?"

Biju shrugged. "That department has some type of investigative arm to respond to crimes. There were a few detectives from the job who went to work as community investigators." Biju shook his head. "That's all I know. I'm not really sure how this whole insane system works."

Finn fumbled with the phone case attached to his belt. "Well, then," he remarked as his iPhone rose to his ear. "I guess I should notify 311."

...

May 29th: Finn tapped his desk with a pen as he studied the weekly payroll summary. A minor detail he had overlooked in his planning was the fact that the homeowners association paid his company monthly. Finn had no capital reserves to cover a month of salaries, and he would have instantly lost his entire security force if he announced that they would have to wait a month to get paid. Once again, Finn's dad bailed him out. Patrick floated Finn a loan to cover payroll and operating costs for two months.

Finn thought he had everything figured out down to the penny, but after just a few weeks of operations, unforeseen expenses seemed to be eating into the only viable source of revenue – his salary. If the present trend continued, Finn would soon find himself the second lowest paid worker in the company. Only Kevin would have a lower salary, and he was being paid minimum wage.

Finn's financial woes were interrupted by the figure in the doorway. With his rumpled appearance in wrinkled khaki trousers, brown unpolished shoes, stained blue shirt unbuttoned at the collar, and blue Yankees baseball cap, Finn was about to direct the visitor to the maintenance office on the next block. There was something familiar about this unkempt, stocky, middle aged man, however, that provided Finn a reason to pause and search the recesses of his memory.

"How you doing?" the voice greeted from the doorway. "I'm Paul Taggart....."

Before the visitor could complete his introduction, Finn slammed his fist on the desktop. "That's it!" he declared. "Paul Taggart!"

The male was obviously not experiencing the same epiphany as Finn. "Yeah, that's me," he chuckled. "Although I can't remember my name ever generating a response like that."

Finn stood behind his desk. "Detective Paul Taggart. You don't remember me? Finn Delaney?"

Paul wagged his right index finger at Finn. "You're Chief Delaney's kid, right?"

"That's right," Finn nodded. "You helped me with the case file on that Demon murder case in Alley Pond Park last year when you were working with the 111th Precinct Detective Squad."

"Yeah, that's right. You did some great work on that getting that innocent kid out of jail."

"Thanks," Finn mumbled.

"And how could I forget the party for that kid." Paul's smile grew wider. "Some huge Amazon girl beat the crap out of some big red headed mope – threw him through a table if I remember correctly."

"You remember correctly," Finn laughed. "That was my friend Kevin who landed on the table."

"Yeah, that was some night," Paul reflected. "How is the chief doing?"

Finn shrugged. "As good as can be expected. He wasn't planning on retiring, but at least he had that option – not like thousands of other guys on the job who didn't have enough time in for a pension." Finn then realized he may have been addressing one of those unfortunates. "How about you, Paul. How are you making out?"

Paul raised his eyebrows. "I don't know. I guess I have to consider myself very fortunate. I'm gonna be able to finish out my last few years and leave with a full pension."

"How is that possible?" Finn queried.

"Me and a handful of other detectives got retained in the Mayor's Community Action Network."

"Is that the same as the Community Response Network?"

"Yeah, yeah," Paul waved his hand dismissively. "Response – action – whatever the hell it's called, I was assigned as an investigator."

"Well, I'm happy for you, Paul. What brings you here today?"

Paul looked confused. "You reported a burglary, didn't you."

Finn slapped his forehead. "That's right. How could I forget. It's the only thing that's happened here."

"Well," Paul shrugged. "I'm your assigned investigator."

"How many investigators are there?" Finn asked.

"Not many," Paul responded. "I am one of four investigators who cover the entire borough of Queens."

"Wow," Finn wailed. "Your caseload must be enormous."

"Not really," Paul sighed.

"How is that possible," Finn snapped, "with only four investigators for the entire borough?"

"You're missing the point, kid," Paul scoffed. "This incompetent mayor says crime is way down, so we don't need many criminal investigators."

"Crime is down?" Finn questioned.

"That's what the statistics say."

"So, what's the real story," Finn probed.

"The real story is that no one is reporting crimes anymore. They don't see the point. A guy gets robbed at gunpoint in the street he just thanks his lucky stars that he wasn't killed and goes home. The only action being taken are by communities like this. They create their own castles – walling themselves in to protect themselves from the invaders."

Paul smirked. "And I can't say that I blame them. So, even though crime is completely out of control, the mayor says we are all living together peacefully as brothers and sisters while I investigate the very few crimes occurring in this peaceful city." Paul shook his head. "What a joke!"

"Are there such things as arrests, anymore?" Finn asked.

"Sure," Paul shot back. "Don't you remember your criminal procedure law?"

"Not really," Finn shrugged.

"That's alright," Paul chuckled. "It's not really important anymore." He took a deep breath. "Police officers used to make arrests based on a standard of proof called probable cause. That meant that the cop had to reasonably believe that an offense was committed and that the person being arrested probably did it." Paul's eyes widened. "Do you see the wording, Finn – reasonable to believe – probably did. The cop could be wrong but it could still be a perfectly legal arrest under the probable cause standard of proof."

"And probable cause is gone?" Finn surmised.

"The dinosaurs, the NYPD, and probable cause – all extinct," Paul declared.

"But you said there were still arrests," Finn remarked.

"Of course," Paul countered. "Private citizens always had, and still do have arrest authority. The private citizen standard of proof to make an arrest is called in fact committed. That means that the person being arrested must be the one who in fact committed the offense – there can be no mistake."

"Well," Finn shrugged. "The only way I can think of that I would be absolutely sure that someone committed a crime was if I saw him do it."

"You're learning kid," Paul smiled. "If you didn't see it, it didn't happen."

Finn was still confused. "So how can you make arrests on cases you investigate after the fact?"

"I usually don't," Paul smirked. "Unless I get a confession, I let it go. Even if I build an airtight case with physical evidence, I'm not going to run the risk that the perp. Is found not guilty at a trial leaving me open to a charge of false arrest."

"That's crazy," Finn remarked.

"This is the world we live in," Paul replied. "Now, let's get into your burglary."

Finn scanned the block after they exited the office. "We may have to walk. My admirative guy went to gas up the patrol car. Wait a minute," Finn corrected himself, "here he comes now."

Paul smiled. "It looks just like an NYPD RMP."

Kevin popped out of the driver's door. "Are you going somewhere, general? Do you want me to leave it running?"

Finn had heard more than enough of Kevin's 'general' quips, but before he could address him, Paul sounded off. "Hey, aren't you the guy who got thrown through the table at that party by that huge girl."

Kevin grimaced and grabbed his back. "That's me. I get a shooting pain in my back every time I think about that beast."

Finn pushed past Kevin to the driver's door. "Enough about your back. We're going over to the vicinity of the Sherman's house on Markwood."

"Yes general," Kevin snapped to attention.

"You better knock off the general crap," Finn whispered before slamming the door shut.

Finn made a right turn at the corner and began describing some of the beautiful homes and attractions in the community. Paul, however, was not the least bit interested in the scenery. "You make them call you general?" he snickered.

Finn grit his teeth. "Don't listen to anything that moron says. He deserves to be thrown through another table."

Finn turned onto Markwood Place and waved. From a chair on her front porch, Candice Rothchild smiled and waved enthusiastically.

"What a nice old lady," Paul commented.

"She is," Finn confirmed. "And she's actually the reason I'm here."

Paul shifted in his seat and looked at Finn. "How's that?"

"I knew the woman and her son from my private investigator business. When she moved into the community, her son became friendly with the homeowners association, and when they decided to form their own public safety department, the son recommended me."

"Good deal," Paul nodded.

Finn pointed ahead and to the right. "There's the Sherman's house. They both work so no one is home right now, but we can still take a look around outside. I also have copies back at the office of every delivery person and contractor the Sherman's could remember for the last month, and the visitor log from the guard booths for three days before the burglary."

"That's great," Paul responded, "but the burglar did not enter through any gates."

"He climbed the fence?" Finn asked.

Paul shook his head. "No, that barbed wire is a pretty good deterrent."

"Then how?"

"Right there!" Paul pointed to the gates at the end of Markwood Place."

"But those gates have always been here. They were here before the fence and other gates were installed and they are always kept locked."

"That doesn't matter," Paul crowed. "Anyone can see it."

"See what?" Finn blurted.

"Come on," Paul suggested. "I'll show you."

The two wrought iron swing gates were attached to a brick wall that ran for ten feet on both sides of the gates. The new chain link fence was tied into the brick wall on both sides and a chain and padlock kept the two gates closed and locked.

Paul shook his head. "You still don't see it? You're kidding."

Finn shrugged as Paul placed his arm in the space between the two gates. "Look at how much space there is here. A skinny kid like you could get through there with no problem."

Finn stroked his chin. "I think you may be right."

"I know I'm right," Paul grinned. "I'm not about to try it, but I'll bet I could wiggle my fat ass through that opening."

"Let's not go crazy," Finn chuckled.

In the end, Paul Taggart took his photos and compiled his notes along with the copies Finn had provided. This was destined to be another unsolved crime in the new City of New York.

...

May 31st: Finn cupped his hands over his mouth and stared at his laptop's screen. His morning ritual had turned into an exercise in depression. As soon as he arrived in the public safety office he would fire up his lap top and check on his payroll and expenses. Finn was smart enough to realize how important it was for him to keep on top of this aspect of the business, still, each day was more depressing as he watched the expenses rise while his salary shrunk.

This morning's depression had two prongs, and Finn wasn't sure which prong was more troublesome. The figures displayed on his screen were bleak, but just as dismal was the scene on the other side of the office. Kevin had his feet up on the desk while happily paging through a professional wrestling magazine.

Finn turned away from his gloomy financial outlook to address his administrative assistant. "Don't you have anything productive to do?"

Kevin looked annoyed at having his reading interrupted. "What?"

"If you are going to drain my salary, can't you actually do some work?"

Kevin threw down the magazine and stood at attention. "Awaiting your orders, general."

Finn fought his instinct to explode. Instead, he took a deep breath and closed his laptop. "Let's take a walk," he smiled.

"Whatever you say, general."

"Wait a minute," Finn called before Kevin reached the office door. "We're supposed to be setting an example in the community," he explained as he flipped a packaged surgical mask to Kevin.

"Where are we going, general?" Kevin asked as he followed Finn's right turn on the sidewalk.

"Over past Flagpole Park," Finn sighed. "I wanted to talk to you about constantly calling me general."

Kevin slapped Finn's back lightly. "Aw, come on. You know I'm just breaking your balls."

"Yeah, I know you don't mean anything by it, but you have to appreciate my position."

Kevin was confused. "What are you talking about?"

"I'm the boss here, and you're making me look like a joke to the rest of the security staff."

Kevin waved a dismissive hand. "You're being way to sensitive, Finbar. The guys know I'm kidding."

Finn stopped. "That's not the point," he moaned. "Please, just do me a favor an knock off the general crap."

"Sure thing gen...." Kevin punched Finn's arm. "I mean Finn."

As they navigated the sidewalk adjacent to Flagpole Park, Finn held up his left hand. "Wait a minute, Kev, I want to say hello to someone."

Finn and Kevin strolled onto the grass and approached the woman performing slow, deliberate stretching movements. "Good morning, Ms. Rothchild. beautiful day, isn't it?"

Candice Rothchild arched her back and smiled. "It certainly is a beautiful day, Mr. Delaney." She stood on her right foot while grabbing her left ankle with her left hand. "And good morning to you, Kevin. So nice to see you again."

Finn's voice was filled with surprise. "You two know each other?"

"Oh yes," Candice replied as she stretched her right leg in a similar manner. "Kevin has been running errands for me whenever I ask. He is such a

sweetheart, isn't he?"

Finn glared at Kevin through squinting eyes. "yeah, he's a real sweetheart."

Candice completed her stretch and held up her right hand toward Finn. "Excuse me for a moment, Mr. Delaney, but I want to make sure Rosa sees me."

Finn took a step to the side and made a quick about face, catching a glimpse of the female entering the park. Rosa wasn't beautiful in the classical way with no flowing golden curls, ivory skin, or piercing eyes of green. This twenty-something with dirt blond hair was shorter than average and certainly larger than a catwalk model. Still, in her ordinariness, Finn found something attractive about her. Something seemed to radiate from within her.

Candice waved for Rosa to join the trio. "Come Rosa, I want you to meet my friend." She pointed to Finn. "This is Mr. Delaney. He oversees the public safety department in the community."

Finn smiled and nodded. "It's a pleasure to meet you, miss."

Rosa returned the smile. "It's my pleasure, sir." she replied in a distinct Eastern European accent.

Finn was a bit puzzled when no introduction of Kevin was forthcoming. His perplexed state transitioned to complete bewilderment when Rosa pulled down her mask, threw her arms around Kevin and planted a big kiss on his lips.

Finn was speechless as Candice explained. "Rosa works for me. I'm in good health, thank the Lord, but at my age there are certain things I need help with." Candice smiled in Rosa's direction. "My late husband left me pretty well off financially, but it never really occurred to me until this pandemic and the craziness in this city that you really can't take it with you."

Finn tilted his head slightly. "I'm not really sure what you mean?"

"I love my son," Candice continued, "but Ben has his family and job in Virginia. He was against me buying this house, but it occurred to me that I did have the money to move into this community, so why shouldn't I make myself feel safer." Candice took a deep breath. "Then it occurred to me that I also had the money to afford to get someone to help me, so I hired Rosa to help me Monday through Friday from 9am to 9pm. She's been a godsend for me."

"That's great," Finn remarked as the puzzle pieces in his head began to fit together. "I take it that Kevin met Rosa while he was running errands for you."

"That's right," Candice winked. "and they seem to be getting along very, very well. Well," candice sighed, "We have to be getting back to the house."

Finn nodded as he glanced at the kanoodling couple. "Yeah, we need to be getting back to the office too. Let's go, Kev."

Kevin pulled back after a final kiss. "call you later, babe,"

"Ok," Rosa beamed.

When he was sure they were out of earshot, Finn began the inquisition. "Ok, what was that all about?"

Kevin grinned. "What's wrong?"

"What's going on with you and that girl?"

Kevin extended his arms to the side. "What can I say. She fell for the big guy's charming personality. After all, she only human."

Finn wagged his finger at Kevin. "I don't like it."

Kevin appeared genuinely surprised. "What don't you like? She's a nice girl. Have I done something wrong?"

Finn took a deep breath. He hated to admit it, but Kevin was right. There was nothing really wrong with him seeing a girl working in the community. Still, this was Kevin, and he had years of experience understanding how situations with his buddy usually ended. "You're right," Finn conceded. "She seems like a nice girl and I wish you lots of luck." He shook his head and stared in Kevin's eyes. "But somehow, I just know that your relationship with Rosa is going to end of giving me a tremendous headache."

Kevin waved off Finn's premonition. "You're really starting to lose it, Finbar. What's wrong, not getting enough loving from Meg?"

"Leave Meg out of this," Finn warned. "Just worry about yourself and your job."

Kevin shrugged. "Whatever you say."

"Now," Finn cleared his throat. "let's take a walk over to the Station Square gate. Biju told me that the entrance lane arm was sticking." Finn placed his right hand on his forehead. "It's another potential headache. If that gate needs to be repaired, that's more money I have to lay out."

"Why?" Kevin snapped. "That's not your gate."

"I know" Finn sighed, "but it's in the contract. I'm responsible for the maintenance of the entry gates."

Kevin shook his finger at Finn. "I'm sorry to say it, but this is a good lesson for you, Finbar."

"What lesson?"

"You should have let me read that contract before you signed it."

Finn stood silently with his mouth wide open. Finally, he shook his head and began walking. "Whatever, let's get over to that gate."

"Sure thing, general," Kevin sang.

Finn stamped his left foot on the sidewalk. "What did I just tell you," he cried.

"Sorry, sorry," Kevin apologized. "I'm trying. I just might slip up once in a while. After all, you do look very general-like with that uniform and those stars. You should be proud."

"Will you just shut up," Finn grumbled.

CHAPTER 7: A TRAGIC ACCIDENT?

June 10th: Finn opened his eyes and yawned. He carefully rolled onto his side and looked at the figure sharing the bed. Meg was a pretty girl, but her soft features appeared even softer in sleep. She looked peaceful, wanting nothing more than to curl up into the curve of his body.

Finn repeated his yawn as he rotated his head to work out the stiffness in his neck. He had been in Meg's room many times, but had never really taken the time to appreciate it. The room was far from elegant but it was full of warmth. On the back wall was a mural - a tree with every color of fall leaf imaginable and a few more besides. At the foot of the pine bed was a hand embroidered orange and blue cover honoring Meg's beloved Mets. From every wall smiled black and white photographs of Meg as a child with her mother and father.

Finn shot up to a sitting position at the sound of the front door.

"What's the matter?" Meg groaned. "Lay down."

"There's someone downstairs," Finn blurted.

Meg rolled over and pulled the blanket up to her neck. "That's just my parents, now lay down."

Finn turned and pulled the blanket down past Meg's waist. "You said your parents weren't coming home until tomorrow morning."

Meg grabbed the blanket and pulled it up again. "They texted me last night and said they were coming home a day early. What's the big deal?"

"What's the big deal?" Finn gasped. "I'm up in your room in bed with you and your parents are here."

"Oh my God, Finn," Meg laughed. "We're twenty-six years old. I think my parents know what we're doing." Meg leaned forward and grabbed both of Finn's shoulders, "Now lay down please."

Once Finn was prone Meg transitioned from grasping his shoulders to a passionate embrace. "That's my good boy," she whispered while she worked her way along his neck with soft kisses.

Knock – Knock – Knock

Finn was stunned, but Meg handled the knocking calmly. "Come in,"

Finn pulled the blanket up to his nose so that just his eyes were exposed.

Janice Hogan stuck the top half of her body through the door. "Just wanted to let you know we're home, dear."

"Thanks mom."

Janice retreated from the doorway, but before the door closed her head poked back in the room. "Oh, hi, Finn." She smiled. "Good to see you again."

"Nice to see you too, Mrs. Hogan," Finn stammered.

The door closed and there was silence in the room. Finn turned and looked at Meg, his eyes as wide as silver dollars. Meg tried to restrain herself but there was no way she was going to stifle her laughter. Her laughter was so free and pure, so childish despite her age. It came to Finn's ears as a tickle and bounce - and he had no choice but to join in such generous mirth.

The vibration on the night table terminated Finn's guffaws. He reached as far as he could and grabbed his iPhone. "What's up Sahib?"

"You need to get over here."

"Come on, Sahib," Finn moaned. "I told you I was taking off today. It's the first day off I've taken since we opened."

Biju's response was solemn and firm. "Finn, you need to get over here right now – please."

Finn sat up in the bed and sighed. "I'll be there in twenty minutes."

...

Finn placed his hands on his hips as he stood in the middle of the empty public safety office. His phone was quickly to his ear. "I'm in the office – where are you?"

Biju's voice was still somber "Meet me at the Rothchild house on Markwood."

When Finn turned the corner onto Markwood Place, he was faced with a curious scene. He didn't know exactly what was happening, but he knew it couldn't be good. The patrol car was parked at a weird angle to the curb as if the operator had rushed the park job to get into the house quickly. On the lawns of the two adjacent homes, neighbors gathered in small, quiet conversation clusters.

The siren jolted Finn out of his analysis. It wailed like a baby in distress – the kind of noise that made Finn feel sick. The queasiness in his stomach only increased when he caught sight of the flashing lights in his rear-view mirror. Finn exited his car and watched the EMTs gather their equipment. He turned toward the house and saw Biju standing in the doorway, waving for him to come in.

Biju stepped out to the porch and met Finn at the top step. "It's not good, Finn. There was an accident."

"What accident?"

Biju nodded toward the interior of the home. "Mrs. Rothchild." He bit his lip and looked toward the street, searching for the right words."

Finn grabbed Biju's forearm. "What happened to Mrs. Rothchild?"

"She's dead!" Biju blurted.

From the living room came the most hysterical crying, the screaming sobs only interrupted by the person's need to draw breath. It was a primal sound; one Finn was programmed not to ignore. Finn rushed past Biju and into the living room. Sean Muldoon was crouched next to the sofa, unsuccessfully trying to comfort Rosa. Finn gazed at the torment in the girl's eyes. Even in the midst of the pain, Finn could not help but notice the beauty of the room. The couch was maroon and looked more like a show piece than a place for sitting. The white curtains were linen, the kind of white that was untouched by hands and devoid of dust., and the floor was a high polished wood, dark and free of either dust or clutter.

Biju came up behind Finn. "She came to work this morning and found Mrs. Rothchild floating in the bathtub upstairs. Apparently, she had an accident in the tub and drowned." Biju shrugged. "Maybe she just had a heart attack. She was pretty old."

Rosa seemed to be gaining some degree of composure until she saw Finn in the room. Her breathing became rapid and labored and her words were mixed with sobs. "Oh my God, this isn't happening! I left last night and Mrs. Rothchild told me she was going to take a late bath. I said I would stay to help her but she insisted that I leave. I came back this morning and she didn't answer the door. I used the key she gave me and went upstairs." In the battle between the words and the sobs, the sobs prevailed. No more words were possible as Rosa buried her head in her hands.

Finn turned his attention back to Biju. "Did you call 911?"

"911?", Biju scoffed. "Sure, I called 911 and they connected me to the immediate community assistance department of 311. They said they would notify the medical examiner and an ambulance."

"What about her son?" Finn inquired. "Has anyone called Ben?"

Biju looked to the floor. "You know him. I figured that would be your job."

Finn turned his attention to the noise on the stairs.

"Here comes the medical examiner," Biju remarked.

Finn watched the doctor make his way down the stairs. He had a face like some guy you'd ask directions on the street. His movements were unhurried and deliberate. Biju motioned for the doctor to approach. "Doctor Martin, this is Finn Delaney, the director of public safety."

"Hello doctor," Finn nodded.

Dr. Martin's voice was deep and he spoke with no jargon. "All indications reflect an accidental drowning. It's a fairly straightforward case. An 85-year old woman alone in the house taking a bath experiences some distress and drowns."

"What kind of distress, doctor?" Finn probed.

"Look," Dr. Martin's voice contained a touch of annoyance. "I found fluid in her lungs. My tests only show that she was in the water. He shrugged. "The cause of death could be unrelated — including heart attack, stroke or allergic reaction — but without signs of foul play, like signs of struggle, such as bruising, to indicate that a person was held underwater, I will consider the death an accidental drowning." Doctor Martin took a step towards the door, but turned back to Finn. "And I saw no signs of foul play upstairs."

Doctor Martin followed the EMTs and the body bag out of the house. Sean and Biju had returned Rosa to a semi-composed condition in the living room. Finn could wait no longer. He knew what he had to do. Finn wandered out to the porch and sat on the front steps. The warm morning breeze felt good, yet, he was shaking. Finn could feel his pulse pounding in his temples as he pressed the phone to his ear.

"Ben, it's Finn Delaney."

"Hey, how's the public safety director," Ben mused

Finn remained solemn. "I'm afraid I have some very bad news, Ben?"

"What are you talking about, Finn?"

Finn gulped deeply before delivering the final shot. "There was an accident in your mother's house. I'm afraid her injuries were too severe and she passed away. I'm so sorry, Ben."

"How, what, what happened?"

"She had an accident while she was taking a bath last night. Her aid found her in the tub this morning."

"Oh my God!" Ben moaned.

"Is there anything you want me to do right now, Ben?"

"No, I'll be there in a half hour."

Ben's response surprised Finn. "A half hour? From Virginia?"

"I'm in New York. I had a deposition on a case in Manhattan yesterday."

"Ok," Finn acknowledged. "So, I'll see you in thirty minutes."

Finn took a deep breath and closed his eyes, attempting to take a mental break from the chaos, if only for a moment. His eyes opened to the image of a mop of red hair bobbing up and down on Markwood Place. His feet pounded the sidewalk with all the grace of a sack of wet concrete. As he turned up the walkway he wheezed as if his lungs were gasping for air. His legs looked unsteady as he bent forward with his hands on his knees, trying to muster enough breath to converse.

"Some shit, huh?" Kevin managed to mutter.

"You said it," Finn replied. "It's good you're here. Rosa is really out of it. You should get her out of here."

"Where is she?"

"In the living room – Biju and Sean are with her."

Kevin patted Finn's shoulder as he passed him. "Ok, buddy, see you later."

Finn still had to wait for Ben Rothchild, and it suddenly occurred to him that he had not been to the scene of the accident. With Kevin now consoling a freshly hysterical Rosa, Finn climbed the stairs and trudged down the long hallway.

Finn was a bit surprised to see that in a house so beautiful, the bathroom could be described as somewhat dilapidated. The formica peeled from the vanities and the enamel was chipped in the sink. But it was scrupulously clean, the old tarnished mirror sparkled and the bath, though also chipped, was as brilliant white as any in a showroom. The floor was dry and the tub drained of water. A wry smile appeared on his face. He knew very little about homicide investigations, but he knew the basics about protecting a crime scene, and this bathroom had been quickly wiped clean of any physical evidence by any number of people – Rosa, Dr. Martin, the EMTs. He shook his head. This better have been an accident. Finn turned to return to the hall, but his eyes shot back to the bathroom. He noticed something. It may be nothing but his eyes kept returning to it. Finn convinced himself that he had watched too much CSI, yet, his eyes kept returning to one area in the bathroom.

CHAPTER 8: THE PUZZLE PIECE

June 12th: Finn felt extremely uncomfortable as he walked down Queens Boulevard. He had not been to any funerals during the pandemic, but he knew from the news media that there were severe restrictions placed on attendance. Ben Rothchild had texted him the details of his mother's service, so he felt obligated to attend, regardless of how uncomfortable he felt.

Finn was elated when he spied Ben off in the distance standing alone on the sidewalk puffing on a cigarette. When Ben saw Finn approaching he flipped the cigarette to the curb and moved in for a social distance violating embrace.

"Thanks for coming, Finn."

"No problem, Ben. It's the least I can do." Finn pointed to the Temple Emmanuel Chapel sign on the building. "I'm glad I saw you out here. I didn't know if I would be allowed in with all the restrictions in place."

Ben shook his head. "You're right. Jewish tradition dictates that burials are to take place as soon as possible after a loved one dies. However, securing a rabbi during these times is difficult." Ben pointed to the surgical mask pulled down on his neck. "They only let a maximum of 10 people in the room, spaced a minimum of six feet apart."

"When is the burial?" Finn asked.

"In about thirty minutes," Ben snickered.

"What?"

"You heard me right," Ben scoffed. "And before the casket is lowered into the ground, Jewish tradition dictates that family members take a shovel full of dirt and place it on top of the casket. The funeral director told me we will be given black latex gloves, and each of us will gather handfuls of dirt to place on the casket in lieu of using a communal shovel."

"It's tough you can't follow your traditions," Finn remarked.

"That's not the worst of it," Ben continued. "After a Jewish funeral, Jews enter into Shiva period when it is customary to visit the home of the bereaved, offer comfort and recite the Mourner's Kaddish." Ben's eyes became moist. "There will be no Shiva. We will all simply return to our individual homes feeling empty and sad."

Finn sighed. "I'm sorry, Ben."

Ben grabbed Finn's hand. "Oh, that's alright. I guess I'm just feeling sorry for myself. Mom lived a good long life and according to the funeral director, we're lucky."

"Luckly?" Finn questioned.

"The funeral director told me that up until about a week ago many Jewish families could not even enter their cemetery due to this pandemic. Only the gravediggers and funeral workers could bury the deceased."

Finn took a deep breath. "Ben, I know this is a horrible time to bring this up, but I wanted to ask you what you know about Rosa, the home aid?"

"Not much. Why do you ask?"

"I don't know," Finn shrugged. "It's just that I saw something odd."

Ben grabbed Finn's hand again and squeezed. "I know you mean well, Finn, but please let my mother rest in peace."

"I'm sorry, Ben. I won't say anything more." Finn cleared his throat. "Could you just do me one small favor?"

"Sure, what is it?"

"When you go through your mother's possessions, let me know if you find any of her property missing."

"Ok," Ben sighed. "I don't know what you're trying to prove, but I'll let you know."

"Thanks, now I'm gonna see if I can get inside to pay my respects."

...

June 14th: Finn sat at his desk performing his least favorite task – analyzing company expenses and payroll. Everything and everyone from Biju, to George Whitman, to his father ensured Finn that all would be okay, but he was still anxious. It came like an electrical storm in his brain that was physically painful. It was different from a headache in that there was a feeling of intense sorrow, like his fears were a type of frozen panic with nowhere to go.

"What's up?"

"You're late!" Finn grumbled.

"Hey," Kevin snapped. "Have a heart. I was talking to Rosa. She's still all broken up over what happened."

Finn closed his laptop. "What do you know about her, other than what it's like to get in her pants?"

"You need to work on your stand-up routine, Finbar," Kevin grunted, "because that's not funny."

"Not funny?" Finn scoffed. "That's a strange comment from the high priest of ha-ha. I thought everything was funny to you."

"Well," Kevin snarled. "Some things just aren't funny, and this is one of them."

Finn opened his laptop again. "Whatever you say, buddy."

Kevin faced Finn with his hands on his hips. "Just what the hell is your point."

Finn closed the laptop again before it had powered up. "My point is that you don't really know anything about that girl, do you?"

"So?"

"So, everyone is accepting so easily that it was a tragic accident that killed Mrs. Rothchild."

"And it wasn't an accident?" Kevin questioned.

Finn pointed his finger at Kevin. "All I'm saying is that girl was the last person to see Mrs. Rothchild alive and the first to find her dead – and I saw something very strange inside that bathroom."

"What did you see," Kevin challenged.

Finn held his right hand up in a stop sign. "That's all I'm gonna say. Just be careful with her."

Kevin began to turn away. "That's screwed up!"

"Screwed up?" Finn blurted. "Let's see, in the past two years your female conquests have included a Satan worshipper, a wrestler who threw you through a table, and a lady who made you dress up like Sherlock Holmes. Is it that far-fetched to think that you've gotten yourself hooked up with a murderer?"

"I'm going home!" Kevin declared.

"No, you're not," Finn retorted. "I have work for you. You might as well earn the salary you're taking from me."

Kevin continued to the door. "I don't feel good – I'm sick."

When the office door closed behind him, Finn raised his voice to make sure Kevin could still hear him. "If your symptoms are COVID related, don't come back for 14-days. And I'm not paying you for this time!"

The office door partially opened revealing a hand with the middle finger extended.

Any response to Kevin's parting gesture was preempted by the vibrating phone dancing on the desktop. It sounded like an annoyed rattlesnake as Finn scooped the device from the desk and raised it to his ear.

"Hello."

"Hi Finn, it's Ben."

"Hey Ben, how are you doing?"

"You know," Ben sighed. "It's tough but I'm hanging in there."

"That's all you can do," Finn agreed.

Ben cleared his throat. "I'm calling about what you asked me."

Finn was momentarily perplexed. "What did I ask you?"

"You don't remember?" Ben chuckled. "About looking to see if any of my mother's property was missing."

"Oh, sure," Finn recalled. "I remember."

"Well," Ben began, "I looked around the house and sure enough I discovered something was missing"

"Really?"

"Yes," Ben continued. "Some of her jewelry is gone."

"What type of jewelry?"

"You have to understand, Finn," Ben cautioned. "I don't know every piece of jewelry mom had, but I know for a fact she had four diamond rings and these rings are missing."

"Do you have any idea of the value of the rings?"

"Each ring is worth at least two thousand dollars."

"And you're sure your mom had these rings," Finn pressed. "She couldn't have sold them without you knowing."

"No, Finn," Ben explained. "That's why I can speak on these particular rings. Mom liked them so much she kept them displayed on the top of her dresser, and I distinctly remember seeing them on her dresser when I was in the house the week before she passed."

"Ok, Ben. Thanks very much for the information."

"What are you thinking, Finn. What's happening?"

"I'm not sure yet," Finn remarked. "But I will keep you updated on anything I find out."

Finn immediately scrolled through his phone contacts and placed the phone back to his ear. There had been an explosion in his brain, but this was not the exploding headache he developed from analyzing his expenses. This was the good sort - the type that carried an air of excitement.

"Hello."

"Paul?"

"Yeah, who is this?"

"It's Finn Delaney."

"Oh, hey Finn. What's up?"

"Yeah, Paul, I just wanted to check to see if you knew who would be handling the investigation at my place. I'm hoping it's you."

There was a brief silence before Paul Taggart responded. "What are you talking about?"

"There was an elderly woman found dead in her bathtub."

"What woman?"

"Remember when you came to my place for that burglary?" Finn asked.

"Yeah, and?"

"We were driving down the street and an old woman waved to me from her front porch. You said what a nice old lady she was and I told you the story of how her son got me connected to the homeowners association here."

"Yeah, I remember the old lady," Paul conceded.

"Well," Finn continued. "She was found dead in her bathtub."

"That's terrible," Paul remarked, "but what do you want me to do about it."

"I figured someone from your office would get this case to investigate."

"Wait a minute," Paul yawned. "let me grab the daily logs. Ok, what's the name and address of the deceased?"

"Candice Rothchild – 28 Markwood Place."

"Accidental drowning," Paul declared.

"What?"

"Accidental drowning," Paul repeated. "The medical examiner closed the case. Didn't you see the M.E. doctor at the scene."

"Yeah, sure," Finn stuttered. "But I still thought there would be some investigation."

"Think again, kid," Paul chuckled. "This is the new city. Crime is way down, including the murder rate. The Medical Examiner says the old lady had an accident in the tub and that's it – case closed."

"Look, Paul." Finn pled. "There are some things I saw that I don't like."

"Are you a homicide detective now, kid?" Paul laughed.

"No, you're right," Finn admitted, "I don't know anything about homicides but I need help from someone who does. Will you help me, Paul?"

"I don't know, kid," Paul stammered. "I'm really kind of busy here."

"Please, Paul," Finn begged. "Just meet me here one time and after you see the scene you can tell me I'm out of my mind and I'll never bother you again."

Paul sighed. "Ok, I'll do this because I like you, and because your dad was always good to me."

"That's great," Finn chirped. "When can you come by?"

"Tomorrow at noon."

"That's fine."

"By the way," Paul inquired. "Does you staff still call you general?"

"See you tomorrow." Finn disconnected the call. He wasn't about to let the parting comment dampen his feeling of excitement.

...

June 15th: Finn's daily dose of depression was again being enhanced by the presence of his administrative assistant. The problem wasn't anything Kevin was doing, it was what he wasn't doing – talking. Kevin hadn't uttered a word since Finn made the comments about Rosa. This wasn't the first time Kevin had initiated the silent treatment. Over the years, his friend had given him the cold shoulder numerous times for a variety of ridiculous reasons. Finn was just going to have to let Kevin work things out in his own head, but for some reason he found Kevin's silence as he moved around the office, particularly distracting. Finn looked away from his expenses and scanned Kevin for some reaction. The silence seemed to hang in the air like the suspended moment before a falling glass shatters on the ground. Finn expected Kevin to scream, yell, or at least make a comment under his breath, but he did none of those things. Instead he got up and grabbed the keys to the patrol car off the wall and departed the office. Thirty seconds later Kevin returned. When he pushed through the door Kevin was ashen, his lips almost blue. His limbs moved as if some inexperienced person was controlling them, and his eyes were wide, looking right at Finn.

"What's wrong with you?"

Kevin held up an envelope in his left hand and finally broke his silence. "I was going to get gas." He pointed at the door with his right hand. "When I get to the sidewalk some guy walks up to me and hands me this." Kevin shook the envelope. "Do you know what it is?" Kevin moaned.

"I have no idea," Finn replied.

"It's a summons," Kevin cried. "That prick Pete is suing me for $2500."

"Really?" Finn was fighting hard to stifle his laughter.

"That's right," Kevin groaned. "Can you believe it?"

"Actually, I can," Finn shrugged.

"You're all heart, as usual," Kevin scoffed.

"Haven't you been paying him?"

"With what?" Kevin shot back.

"With the salary I pay you, jerk."

Kevin grabbed his forehead. "Oh yeah, that's right. I almost forgot. Your generous minimum wage."

"That's right," Finn sneered. "That salary that I pay you for the job you begged for."

Kevin extended his arms to the side. "How the hell am I going to pay anything to Pete when I have to live on minimum wage?"

"That's your problem," Finn quipped. "Now why don't you gas up the patrol car."

Kevin pushed the door hard as he exited, slamming it against the outside brick wall.

"Hey!" Finn yelled. "Easy with that door. I don't need another repair bill."

The door slightly opened followed by the familiar hand with extended middle finger.

...

"Ben, this is Paul Taggart."

"Nice to meet you detective."

Paul shrugged. "I'm not really a detective anymore, but nice to meet you too." Paul bit his lip. "And I'm very sorry for your loss."

Ben hung his head and slightly nodded. "Thank you."

Paul scanned the living room. "This is a beautiful house."

"It certainly is," Finn agreed. "Should we go up to the bathroom?"

"Wait a minute," Paul cautioned. "Before we get into anything, I just want to explain the reality of this situation."

"That's fine," Finn remarked.

"Why don't we sit," Paul suggested, "while I tell you a story."

"A story?" Finn was puzzled.

"Yeah," Paul adjusted his position on the beautiful sofa. "About ten years ago I caught a case in the 111 Precinct detective squad. A lady in her 40's was found floating in the tub by her husband. These were well to do people who lived in a beautiful house on Shore Road overlooking Little Neck Bay. The husband said he found his wife floating face down, and he pulled her out of the water and performed CPR." A small smile appeared on Paul's face. "The husband also drained the bathtub." Paul cleared his throat, "So, two rookies covering the sector respond to the job and the husband tells them that his wife probably took too much of her bipolar medication and slipped in the bathtub or she committed suicide. The cops didn't rope of the bathroom, and they let the EMTs remove the body from the bathroom floor, and the EMTs even mopped the bathroom floor dry. When the sergeant arrived on the scene he called me and told me that he knew I would have my work cut out for me just by the nature of the death, but that now this case would be next to impossible to prove if it was a homicide."

Paul glanced back and forth between Finn and Ben. "Do you see the point I'm driving at?"

"Not really," Finn shrugged.

Paul took a deep breath and continued. "Homicides by drowning are among the most difficult murders to prove. Evidence can be washed away, collecting forensics can be difficult, and since drowning is common, everyone may assume the death was an accident." Paul addressed Finn. "You said the Medical Examiner was here, right?"

"Yeah," Finn replied. "Dr. Martin."

"Well," Paul explained. "The M.E. will only determine drowning as the cause of death after ruling out all other reasonable possible explanations for why the victim ended up in the water, such as a drug overdose or a heart attack. Complicating the issue is the fact that there is no definitive test to determine that a death was caused by drowning. M.E.s can find fluids in someone's lungs, but those tests only show that the person was in the water. The cause of death could be unrelated, like a heart attack, stroke, or allergic reaction. A proper investigation would look for signs of a struggle on the body and at the scene – things like bruises on the body that would indicate a person was held underwater." Paul leaned back and slapped his thighs. "So, you see how difficult it is to prove this kind of case even when the scene has been preserved."

"Are you telling us this is all a waste of time?" Finn asked.

Paul shook his head. "I'm just being realistic. You already told me this scene wasn't preserved, and the Medical Examiner already classified the death as an accidental drowning." He pointed his right index finger at Finn. "And even if you did uncover some fantastic evidence, a prosecutor would still have to prove at a trial that the drowning was intentional."

"So?" Finn responded.

"So, kid, you're forgetting this brave new world we live in. There are no more police officers in this city meaning there is no more probable cause standard of proof. All arrests are made with the private citizen standard of proof – in fact committed. That means that if I arrest someone it has to be the person who in fact committed the crime – there can't be a mistake. If I make an arrest based on physical evidence and the person gets found not guilty at trial, then he did not in fact commit the crime and I am open to a charge of false arrest." Paul shook his head. "That's not going to happen to yours truly."

Finn threw his arms in the air. "So, how does an arrest ever get made?"

"Hey," Paul replied. "You're welcome to make the arrest. You're a private citizen with as much arrest authority as me."

Finn had a blank look on his face as Paul stood. "Alright, enough of me telling you all the problems – let's go look at the bathroom."

Paul led the way down the second floor hallway. He stopped in the bathroom doorway and turned to Finn. "Ok, what did you see in here?"

Finn approached the doorway and pointed to the left side of the bathroom. The opaque shower curtain was bunched tightly against the wall, leaving almost the entire tub visible.

"Look." Finn pointed to the shower curtain rod. Although it was in place, the hollow chromium bar showed a slight bend at its center. And look at the wall," Finn pointed to a missing screw from one of the end fittings. "And look at the rings," Finn motioned towards the first three rings. The rings were in place around the bar, but a closer inspection revealed that these rings had breaks in them.

Paul smiled and asked a rhetorical question. "So, Sherlock, what do you see here?"

Finn nodded and continued pointing at the curtain. "I see a shower curtain that was ripped down forcefully. At some point, whether it was because she was in distress due to some medical condition or a physical attack, Mrs. Rothchild was flailing her arms and the only thing she could grab was the shower curtain."

"Keep going," Paul prodded.

"When she grabbed the shower curtain, the rod bent, the screws came out, and the first three rings broke."

"That was very observant," Paul praised. "But how did the shower curtain get put back in place."

Finn shrugged, "Who knows? You said it yourself, Paul. Nothing at this scene was protected. It could have been Rosa, the M.E., the EMTs." Finn extended his arms to the side. "For all I know it could have been Biju or one of my guys."

"You're making my point for me, Finn," Paul explained. "You made a great observation. In essence, you found a puzzle piece. The problem is that all the pieces from the rest of the puzzle are gone, so you don't even know if this piece is a part of the puzzle."

"Guilty." Ben Rothchild stood outside the bathroom raising his hand like a student attempting to answer the teacher's question. "I put the shower curtain back in place."

"What?" Finn blurted.

"When I came here that evening, I looked in the bathroom and saw the curtain and rod inside the bathtub." Ben looked down and shook his head. "I don't know why, but I had an impulse to fix the curtain – I guess to restore some sense of normalcy. So, I saw one of the tiny screws on the floor and I straightened the bar as much as I could and put it back up." Ben gulped. "I'm sorry."

"Don't be sorry," Paul declared. "You had a natural reaction. If I was in your position I probably would have done the same thing." Paul glanced at Finn. "I hope you see my point, kid. The horse is out of the barn. Even if this was something other than an accident, all the physical evidence is gone."

Finn sighed deeply. "Then this makes this next piece of information even more frustrating."

"What?" Paul squinted.

"I asked Ben to check to see if any of his mother's property was missing and he told me that four diamond rings are gone."

"Really?" Paul turned to face Ben. "How are you sure she didn't sell them, give them away, or donate them to some charity?"

"No," Ben shook his head. "Like I told Finn, mom loved those particular rings so she kept them out on display on the top of her dresser. I saw the rings on the dresser no more than a week ago."

Paul nodded. "Ok, now we have direct evidence of a theft, but not a murder."

Finn stroked his chin. "I don't understand. Ben said the rings could have been worth more than ten thousand dollars in total. Isn't that a great motive for murder?"

"Sure it is," Paul shrugged. "But what about a simple larceny of opportunity?"

Finn scratched his head. "What are you talking about?"

Paul walked down the hall and stopped in front of the next door. "This is your mom's bedroom, right, Ben?"

"Yes."

Paul pointed to the interior of the room. "And I assume that is the dresser where she displayed the rings?"

"It is."

"Let me ask you, Ben, did your mom always keep the bedroom door closed when she wasn't inside?"

Ben squinted slightly. "No, I don't think so."

Paul waved his arm towards both ends of the hall. "So, anyone going back and forth along this hallway would have been able to see those rings, right?"

"I guess you're right," Finn admitted.

Paul placed his index finger on his temple. "Now, let's look at access. Who could have walked past this room and seen the rings?"

Finn began keeping track of his count on his fingers. "There was Biju, and Sean Muldoon, Rosa the aid, Dr. Martin, the two EMTs."

"Don't forget yourself," Paul added.

"What?" Finn gasped. "I never went upstairs."

Paul grinned. "Then how did you make these great observations?"

Finn inhaled deeply. "You're right, Paul. I guess I had access too."

Paul placed his hand on Finn's shoulder. "Come on, kid, I know you didn't do it, but I'm just making the point of how hard it is to prove one of these cases, even if you have solid physical evidence – which we don't." Paul placed his hand under Finn's chin and lifted it so that Finn was looking in his eyes. "And I know you feel funny about that girl, and that's natural."

"What do you mean?" Finn asked.

"You know the old saying – the butler usually did it."

"Sure."

"Well," Paul nodded. "There's some truth to that saying. Someone who worked for a victim is certainly someone to take a close look at."

"So," Finn shrugged. "What now, Paul?"

"Probably nothing," Paul chuckled. "But I have to admit, you've gotten my juices flowing again. I really miss this detective crap."

Finn continued to probe. "So, what are we going to do."

Paul raised his eyebrows. "Even though it's likely to accomplish absolutely nothing – we talk to the girl."

CHAPTER 9: THE GRIFTERS

June 16th: Finn entered the public safety office to behold an odd sight – Kevin was hard at work. His administrative assistant had papers spread out all over the desk while he furiously scribbled notes on a legal pad.

"What are you doing?" Finn inquired as he slid behind his own desk.

"Working – what does it look like I'm doing," Kevin snapped without looking up.

"Hey, I'm just curious," Finn shot back. "After all, the sight of you at work is like witnessing a full solar eclipse. You may only see it a few times in a lifetime."

Kevin dropped his pen, looked up and frowned. "Can you please not break my balls right now. This is very important and I'm trying to concentrate."

Despite the warning, Finn continued the ball breaking. "Be careful with that concentrating, you don't want to burn out that dim light you have in that brain of yours."

"Very funny."

"Seriously," Finn remarked. "I'm thrilled to see you finally engaged in your job. What are you working on?"

Kevin grabbed one of the papers and held it up. "I'm working on this bullshit lawsuit."

Finn leaned back in his chair. "I knew it!," he scoffed. "I knew you wouldn't be doing actual work – the work I pay you to do."

Kevin had already returned to his scribbling. "Buzz off and let me do this."

Finn was still puzzled. "What are you working on with the lawsuit?"

"My defense," Kevin responded.

"Defense?" Finn roared. "What defense? You're as guilty as sin and you're lucky Pete couldn't figure out how to put you in jail."

"No matter what you say," Kevin replied. "I've given this a lot of thought and I've come up with a great defense."

"And what might that be?"

"That's my business," Kevin snarled as he returned to his legal pad.

•••

Finn watched the rhythm of the wipers gliding across the windshield, wiping away the softly splashing water droplets. The traffic on the Grand Central Parkway adjacent to LaGuardia Airport was unusually light, a direct result of the pandemic, and the resulting lack of airport activity. Finn tired of watching the wipers and switched his view. The skies were overhung with a blanket of grey, so much so that he could barely tell the difference between the sky and clouds. Despite the gloom of the day, Finn found something calming about watching raindrops race down the windows.

"What's the address again?" Paul asked.

Finn pulled out his phone and pressed the screen several times. "Ben got it out of his mother's address book -30-24 28th Street."

Paul activated the right signal and moved into the right lane. "This is our exit. That address is only a couple of minutes away."

"I don't know why we didn't just use GPS?" Finn lamented.

"People depend too much on GPS." Paul replied. "If GPS didn't work one day, I'll bet you wouldn't be able to go anywhere away from your house."

Finn chuckled. "Let's just hope GPS never goes away. By the way," Finn continued. "I just got Rosa's phone number from Ben yesterday. How did you get an interview with her so quickly?"

"Simple," Paul shrugged, "I asked her."

Paul reached the top of the exit ramp and turned left under the elevated subway structure.

"Somehow," Paul began, "Astoria has gotten the reputation of being one of the hippest spots in the city."

"Tell me about it." Finn agreed. "Meg liked coming here pre-COVID."

"And you?" Paul inquired.

"I can take it or leave it," Finn shrugged. "It's always so crowded on weekend nights."

"Well," Paul theorized, "I guess it's easy to see why the cool cats would be drawn here."

"Cool cats?" Finn raised an eyebrow.

"Hipsters, beatniks, whatever you want to call them." Paul nodded toward the street scenes they were passing. "Look at the diversity – the flavor – the energy. I can only imagine how this place is with no pandemic. Just going down this street I've seen an Egyptian restaurant, a hookah bar, and an Irish pub."

"I guess you're right." Finn's voice lacked enthusiasm.

"And look at the buildings," Paul continued. "Look at the mix. Older apartment buildings stand alongside modern residences, and it's the same with restaurants, coffee shops, storefronts, and bars."

Paul turned right onto 28th Street. 30-24 was a dilapidated mess. Finn shook his head as Paul parallel parked. Obviously, the landlord had long ago stopped investing in renovations. The neglect seemed so complete that Finn theorized that it was by design – letting the building fall apart so the land could be sold for construction. This mess certainly looked out of place in between the new glass and steel monoliths on either side that seemed to grow right out of the sidewalk.

When they entered the graffiti-laden lobby, it was no surprise to find the elevator inoperable. The four-story climb was made more complicated by having to step over two drunks laid out on the stairs.

At the fourth-floor landing, Paul had to stop for moment to catch his breath. Finn was not winded, but his knee was twinging enough to annoy him. Something else besides his knee was bothering him. "Hey,

Paul, I know you said you simply asked Rosa to meet you, but why in God's name would she agree to meet with some investigator from the city – especially if she is dirty?"

Paul took a few deep deliberate breaths as his breathing returned to a normal rate. "Well, Finn, I may have told her that she may be eligible for a cash payment for people who lost their jobs during the pandemic."

"Oh, I see," Finn grinned. "You lied."

"Not so fast, kid," Paul wagged his finger. "She may very well be eligible for some benefits. How would I know?"

The only distinguishing features on the door were the chipping paint and unreadable graffiti. Paul knocked sharply three times and waited. The door opened just a crack, then after the sound of a chain being unlatched, it flew open wide.

For some reason Rosa didn't look so pretty to Finn anymore. Maybe it was the sneer on her face or perhaps it was the background in which her frowning face was framed. The apartment wasn't just a mess, it was a disaster zone. It looked to Finn like a drunken cyclone had erupted in the room strewing clothes, furniture, and knick-knacks across the length of the room.

As he stepped inside the apartment Finn's nose immediately wrinkled in disgust. The stench of unwashed clothes and mouse droppings had intermingled, quickly bringing tears to his eyes. Finn stumbled over a misplaced shoe, causing him the stub his big toe on a guitar propped up against the wall. His kick of the untuned guitar produced an eerie, screeching sound that reverberated in his ears.

Finn instantly decided it was in his best interests to remain stationery in this jungle of dirty clothes, uneaten food, and various sized piles of junk. Paul, on the other hand, seemed to be having no problem wading through the mess. He made a complete lap of the room holding a clipboard in one hand and a pen in the other as he mumbled to a confused Rosa something about eligibility for benefits.

"Who are these people?" The voice from the doorway thundered.

"It's alright, Agon," Rosa explained. "This man said I may qualify for some money for working for the lady who died."

"Money?" The man was small and thin, with the long scar running along his right cheek looking terribly out of place on his baby face. He ran his hand through his close-cropped hair three times in quick succession, fixing a stare at Paul that could have frozen a tropical sea. "You are full of shit! Get the hell out of here!"

Paul looked at Rosa. "Who the hell is this guy?"

"This is my Agon – my husband."

When the word husband emerged from Rosa's mouth, Finn accidentally kicked the guitar again, toppling it to the floor. He shook his head – Kevin had done it again.

"I said get out, now!" Agon reached into a pile of junk and pulled out a sawed-off baseball bat.

Paul was not amused. "You should be very careful when you threaten people," he warned as he moved to the doorway. "It's a very easy way to get yourself hurt."

Finn was already in the hall as Paul stepped through the door just as Agon slammed the door shut.

"That went well," Finn remarked as he entered the stairway landing.

Paul nodded. "Actually, that went better than I expected."

"What are you talking about?" Finn asked.

"Paul slapped Finn on the back and started down the stairs. "I'll explain everything later. Just call Ben Rothchild and tell him to meet us at his mother's house."

Finn jumped out of the car when Paul stopped at the curb next to the public safety office. Paul had yet to fully explain what was going on, but he asked Finn to bring his laptop to the Rothchild house. Finn keyed through the office door and strode directly to his desk. He was momentarily startled when he observed Kevin seated at the other desk.

"Still working on your defense?" Finn mocked as he scooped up his computer.

Kevin shook his head. "No, I'm actually doing some work on the schedule. I have to leave early today and I want to finish this so my boss doesn't fire me."

Finn moved towards the door with the laptop tucked safely under his arm. "Why are you leaving early?"

"I'm meeting Rosa for dinner. The poor thing is still all broken up over what happened."

Finn was halfway out the door when his progress came to an abrupt halt. "Hey Kev."

"What?"

Finn took a deep breath but said nothing more than "Don't forget to lock the door when you leave the office." He'd address the Rosa situation with him at some other time.

Ben Rothchild waved from the porch as the car pulled to the curb. Five minutes later Finn sat on the edge of the sofa, flanked on either side by Paul and Ben. Finn stared at the laptop on the coffee table directly in front of him as it ran through its booting process. Paul unscrewed his pen and pulled out a small, thin card. He inserted the card into the back of a flash drive before handing the portable drive to Finn.

"Here," Paul said. "Install this."

Finn inserted the flash drive in the USB port and waited for the drive to activate. "What's on this?" he asked.

"What did you think," Paul chuckled, "that I was walking around that shithole apartment to appreciate the decor."

"No," Finn shook his head, "but I still don't understand."

Finn's inquiry was cut short by the video image that popped onto the screen..

"Oh my God!" Finn blurted. "That pen was a video camera."

"1080p full HD," Paul boasted.

"What an awful looking apartment," Ben remarked.

Paul tapped Finn's forearm. "Stop it there."

Finn's index finger came down on the left click button on the touchpad.

"Do you know how to digitally zoom on that image?" Paul asked.

"I think so," Finn said as he slid his thumb and index finger on the touchpad.

"Right there!" Paul declared. he reached across Finn and tapped Ben's knee. "Does that look familiar?"

Ben leaned forward and to the left to get a good view of the screen. "Oh my God!" Ben whispered.

"What is it?" Finn asked.

Ben pointed at the screen. "That crystal bowl was a wedding gift to my mother and father. See - you can make out their names."

Finn leaned in closer to the screen and nodded. "You're right, Ben. I can make out Candice and Herbert and I think the date is May 3rd, 1960."

Ben sat back in the sofa and nodded. "That was their wedding date." He looked at Paul. "So, the girl is a thief, but is she a murderer too?"

Paul scratched his cheek. "I wouldn't call her a thief. I think grifter would be a better description."

"What's a grifter?" Finn asked.

Paul sat back in the sofa. "Grifters are small-time lawbreakers, not the kind of epic liars who leave the wreckage of lives and nations in their wake. They tend to pilfer just enough to disrupt but not devastate. They're like gypsies. They pull their wagon into town – run their scam, and before you know it they're gone, off to find their next town and victim." Paul could see in Finn's eyes that he still wasn't clear on what a grifter was. "A grifter is a con artist – a scammer – a swindler. Get it?"

Finn recoiled in the sofa. "You got all that from the bowl,"

Paul shook his head. "You were in there with me. Didn't you see all the personal items in amongst all the garbage and junk?"

Finn bit his lip and looked down. He felt a bit foolish that he didn't have the same powers of observation as Paul. He had been more focused on not falling down in that horrible room.

Paul touched Finn's shoulder as non-verbal cue to continue the video. "There was something else I saw that was very significant."

Finn activated the video again, but kept his index finger hovering over the left click button. The image instantly froze when Paul said, "Stop!"

"Zoom in again," Paul instructed. "Do you see that?"

"I do," Ben answered. "It looks like a checkbook."

"It is," Paul clarified. "And the names on the checks were Agon and Roze Lejos." Ben looked at Ben. "Where did your mother find that girl?"

Ben shook his head and sighed. "I don't know. She did everything without me. She bought the house without asking me. I never thought to ask her where she found the girl."

"Don't worry," Paul replied. "It's not important now." He stroked his chin. "What's curious to me is that these scammers are usually not murderers. They would have no problem cleaning your mom out piece by piece, but they usually don't murder - and not for a few rings."

"So, what do we do know?" Finn asked.

"I have no access to crime databases anymore, but I know a detective in Nassau County who will help me run some checks on Agon and Roze Lejos." Paul looked at Finn and smiled. "You know something. You really got my investigative juices flowing again."

...

Finn stood alone next to the Station Square gates. He felt like crying. It had been awhile since he last cried, and he honestly didn't know if he was capable of it anymore. It wasn't that he didn't want to - hell, as his financial hole got deeper and deeper some days he wanted nothing more than to curl up into a ball and have the tears wash away the heaviness in his chest, but he just couldn't. They refused to form, to take shape and make their way silently down his face. Even as he watched Biju direct Tony to raise and lower the gate from inside the booth, no moisture developed in his eyes.

Biju shook his head as he approached Finn. "There's definitely something wrong with the controls for the entrance lane gate. Isn't this the gate we just had fixed?"

"No, that was the exit lane." Finn's voice lacked any emotion.

"I bet that repair was expensive," Biju remarked.

"It was, and I'm sure this gate will be just as expensive," Finn said.

Biju scratched his head. "You sound pretty cool for a guy who said he was drowning in bills."

"I've drowned," Finn shrugged. "So, what's the use of getting worked up over it anymore. I'm screwed and I know it."

Finn took a slow stroll back to the public safety office. He thought the walk might clear his head and help his sour mood. He reached the walkway to the office still engulfed his doldrums, and the yelp from the siren didn't make him feel any better. Kevin jumped out of the patrol car and came up behind him on the walkway.

"Patrol vehicle all gassed up, boss."

"That's just wonderful," Finn sighed as he opened the office door.

"What's your problem now?" Kevin asked as he followed Finn inside and hung the patrol car keys on the peg on the wall.

Finn plopped in his chair and put his feet up on his desk. "Every time I take a step forward, something happens to push me two steps back."

Kevin sat behind the other desk and joined Finn with his feet on the desk. "It will get better, Finbar."

"That's easy for you to say. You're not the one trying to keep this operation above water."

"Well, I think you're doing a great job," Kevin chuckled, "as long as you keep paying me."

Finn stretched his arms to the side and looked at the ceiling. "Real funny – by the way. Why are you in such a good mood? It wasn't long ago that you were giving me the silent treatment."

Kevin waved his hand at Finn, "Ah, that's water under the bridge. I know you don't really have anything against Rosa."

Finn removed his feet from the desk and sat up straight. "How is Rosa?"

"Great," Kevin grinned. "I already told you, we're going out to dinner tonight."

"You're going out to dinner during a pandemic?" Finn questioned.

"Jeez, Finbar," Kevin shook his head. "You're always telling me to keep up with current events. Maybe you should follow your own advice."

"What do you mean?"

"I mean that things are beginning to open up. Outdoor dining was authorized in the city so we're going to Bradley's on Woodhaven Boulevard. They have a really nice outdoor set up."

Finn took a deep breath and cleared his throat. "Kevin, there's something really important I have to talk to you about."

"I'm all ears, buddy."

"Well," Finn wiped his mouth. "You see, it's about...." The vibration caused Finn's phone to perform a dance on the desk. Finn saw Paul Taggart's phone number displayed on the screen, so he immediately terminated his heart to heart conversation with Kevin.

"Excuse me, Kev, I have to take this call." Finn departed the office and leaned up against the hood of the parked patrol car. "Hey, Paul. What's up?"

"Plenty!"

"You found something out? What?"

"My buddy in Nassau County didn't have anything, but he told me about an investigator in the North Carolina State Bureau of Investigation."

"North Carolina?"

"That's right. North Carolina has some of the fastest growing retirement communities – fertile ground for these scammers."

"What did you find out?"

"They have three open cases on Agon and Roze Lejos, all the same M.O."

"What was the M.O.?" Finn asked, feeling somewhat satisfied that he understood the jargon.

"The girl hooks up as an aide for an elderly woman living alone and starts to bilk her of her money an possessions."

"How come they didn't arrest them?"

"Is not as simple as that kid. These con artists usually don't just grab something while the mark isn't looking and stuff it in their pockets – they create a story where the mark gives them the money and property as gifts."

"Really?"

"Sure, there have been some cases where grifters have gotten the mark to sign over houses to them and make them the beneficiary on their will."

"Is that what the goal was here?" Finn asked.

"Maybe, but these two seem like amateurs who will squat in some dilapidated apartment and be content with grabbing crystal bowls and rings before they move on." Paul sighed deeply. "But the thing that sticks in my craw is the murder."

"What do you mean?"

"Slugs like this work their magic through the con – they never get physical. And it's especially curious since it appears that there would have been a lot more besides the crystal bowl and the rings for them to scam out of the old lady."

"Maybe she caught them in the act," Finn theorized.

"Maybe," Paul replied. "In any event, it's probably a moot point."

"What do you mean?"

"They probably packed their bags and were on the run five minutes after we left that hole in the wall."

"Oh no!" Finn's voice rose an octave. "They're still here."

"How do you know?"

"My friend Kevin has been seeing Rosa. He's having dinner with her tonight."

"These people are too much," Paul chuckled. "She's probably got her claws into your friend for whatever she can get."

"Well, at least she's not gonna get much there. He's almost as big a deadbeat as they are."

"Well," Paul laughed. "If your friend still has a dime, she'll try to get it from him."

"So, what do we do, Paul?"

"Where are they going to dinner?"

"Bradley's on Woodhaven Boulevard – outside dining."

"I've been there many times," Paul said. "It's a great place. You don't live too far from there, do you Finn?"

"About five blocks."

"I'll pick you up at 7."

"What are we gonna do," Finn asked.

"You'll see. What's you address?"

•••

Finn sat on his front stoop tossing pebbles at a stick lying in his walkway. He had yet to score a hit on the stick when his game ended at the sound of a car horn. He settled into the passenger seat and clicked the seatbelt closed.

"Ok, Paul, what's the game plan?"

Paul turned toward Finn and smiled. "We ride to the sound of the guns."

"What?"

"The direct approach kid - no beating around the bush. We go right at her and see what happens."

As he strolled with Paul along Woodhaven Boulevard, Finn gazed skyward. The cloudy night brought a twilight feel long before the sun was ready to set. The warm breeze had a dampness to it that wasn't there a short while ago – it was cooler and fresher too. "It must be tough on these outdoor dining set-ups when it starts raining."

"I'm sure it is," Paul replied.

Off in the distance Finn could see the green awning of Bradley's Pub. Bradley's was on the corner of Woodhaven Boulevard and 63rd Street, and as they drew closer Finn could see the dining arrangements. The curbside lane on the south side of 63rd street was partitioned by a plywood barricade that ran for about 100-feet. Inside the barricade eight socially distanced tables sat under green and white umbrellas. All the tables were occupied, but it didn't take Finn long to spot the mane of red hair sticking up higher than the rest of the diners.

"There they are," Finn pointed.

"Ok," Paul nodded. "Follow me."

"There's about a thirty minute wait," the smiling hostess reported at the podium outside the dining area.

"That's ok, honey," Paul remarked. "We're meeting people."

As Finn followed Paul into the dining area he caught a look into Kevin's unsuspecting eyes. "Poor bastard," he mumbled.

Paul plopped into the seat next to Rosa while Finn moved in next to Kevin.

"What a surprise," Paul gushed. "You don't mind us joining the party, do you?"

Rosa's eyes were wide with rage. "What are they doing here?" she fumed at Kevin.

Kevin turned to Finn. "What the hell is going on here?"

Finn remained silent while Paul continued the dialogue. "There's nothing wrong with some quality time with friends, is there?"

Rosa stood and reached for Kevin's hand. "Let's get out of here, babe."

Paul reached into the basket for a breadstick. "Leaving so soon. That's too bad. Make sure to say hello to your husband for me."

"Husband?" Kevin blurted. "Will someone please tell me what is going on here."

"Nothing is going on," Rosa claimed as she sat back down and stared at Paul. "And my morality is no business of yours."

"You're absolutely right, darling. I could care less that you are out here cheating on your man."

"Cheating?" Kevin was still in a state of shock.

The breadstick cracked under Paul's teeth. "But a con artist like you who commits larceny, burglary, and murder is my business."

"Murder?" Kevin's voice squeaked and cracked.

"You are insane," Rosa snarled. "I have done nothing illegal."

"Oh, no?" Paul shot back. "How about that crystal bowl in your shitty apartment that was a wedding present to Mrs. Rothchild?"

Rosa smiled. "The lady gave me that bowl as a gift."

"Really?" Paul reached for a roll. "And I suppose she gave you her diamond rings too."

"You really are crazy," Rosa scoffed. "I have no diamond rings."

"Will someone please tell me what is going on here?" Kevin begged.

"You're being fleeced by a con artist, pal," Paul replied.

"What?"

"Don't listen to him, baby," Rosa implored.

"Of course, she doesn't want you to listen to me," Paul chuckled. "Let me ask you something. Are you giving her money tonight?"

"You don't have to tell him anything," Rosa snapped.

Kevin glared at Rosa and then turned his attention to Paul. "I gave her money for a plane ticket so that she could visit her sick mother in Texas."

"That's a good one," Paul nodded.

"You mean she doesn't have a sick mother in Texas?"

"Very doubtful," Paul shrugged. "It's much more likely that after she squeezed every possible penny out of you tonight, your girlfriend and her husband were going to be in the wind to parts unknown to begin running new scams with new victims."

Rosa grabbed Kevin's hand and addressed him with tears in her eyes. "Please don't listen to him. I really like you."

"Are you married?" Kevin asked.

"Well, yes," she gulped. "But I really do like you."

Kevin pulled his hand away and turned away from Rosa. "I heard enough," he groaned.

Rosa's speech was becoming more rapid and frantic. "If you think I'm a crook, then search my apartment, or better yet, search me." She unhooked her pocketbook from her chair and pushed it at Paul. "Here, search my bag – search it!"

Paul swallowed the last morsel of the roll before accepting the handbag. "Ok," he sighed. "If you insist." Paul's right hand fished around inside the bag for about a minute. Finally, his hand emerged rolled up in a fist. He smiled as he held his closed hand out toward Rosa. Slowly his fingers parted revealing four diamond rings laying in the palm of his hand. "That was easier than I thought," Paul snickered.

Rosa completely lost her composure. "I don't know how they got there," she exploded. "You put them there," she pointed menacingly at Paul. "You are trying to set me up."

Paul deposited the rings in his shirt pocket. "Frankly, I'm not really concerned about what you stole. Even a blind man could see that you are a low-life con artist. I'm more concerned with why you murdered the old lady."

"I didn't kill anyone," Rosa hissed.

Paul Nodded. "I don't think you did kill Mrs. Rothchild."

Finn had become increasingly confused watching the action. "She didn't kill her?" Finn said.

"No, she didn't kid. Her husband Agon did."

"How?" Finn asked.

"I believe that on the night of the murder, this wonderful couple had some big score planned. I'm not exactly sure what was going to be taken, but it was something big – something that Rosa didn't want to be seen carrying. Rosa went off duty as normal at 9PM and has the officer at the Station Square gate to verify her departure."

"But how did her husband get in?" Finn asked.

"Did you forget the burglary of the Sherman house," Paul said. "Skinny Agon slipped between the Markwood gates and entered the house with the key Rosa gave him. Something inside went wrong, however. Mrs. Rothchild probably interrupted whatever he was trying to do, so he had no choice but to kill her. He then slipped out the same way he came in – through the Markwood gates."

Rosa shook her head and laughed. "You are completely out of your mind. It's no wonder the police department is gone, with morons like you who were making decisions." She stood as she readied to make her exit. "If you think I murdered that lady, or stole from her house – then arrest me. I dare you."

"Not tonight," young lady," Paul said as he grabbed another breadstick. "Maybe tomorrow, though," he remarked as Rosa slipped behind him.

Paul's comment brought Rosa to a stop. "What do you mean – tomorrow?"

Paul took a bite of breadstick. "I mean, I am going to get something that is going to nail your shapely butt to the wall."

"More lies," she scoffed.

"The Sherman's live across the street from the Rothchild house. Awhile back they were burglarized by a scumbag who got into the community through the open space in those Markwood gates – just like you."

"What's your point, asshole," Rosa snarled.

"Well, the Sherman's learned a lesson after that burglary. They installed a bunch of CCTV cameras, and a couple of those cameras look out to the front of their house." Paul grinned. "In other words, those cameras will show what's going on across the street, including everyone who came in and out of the Rothchild house and anyone sliding through the Markwood gates. The Sherman's have been away, but they are coming home tomorrow morning. I'll review that video sometime tomorrow and then I'm sure we'll be talking again."

"Go screw yourself," Rosa said as she departed the dining area. She turned in the street and returned on the opposite side of the plywood barrier directly adjacent to Kevin. "And you can screw yourself too. How dare you let him talk to me like that."

"That's a class act all the way," Paul nodded as Rosa disappeared down the boulevard.

Kevin held his arms out to the side. "How do I find these women?"

"I don't know," Finn chuckled. "but you sure seem to have a knack for it."

Kevin slammed his hand on the table. "Shit! I just let her walk away with two hundred bucks."

Kevin began to rise but Paul placed his hand on his forearm. "Forget it. She's gone. You'll never see that money again."

"Hey Paul," Finn said. "Do you think it was a good idea to tell her about the video cameras at the Sherman's house."

"I don't know," Paul smiled. "I guess we'll find out, won't we?"

Paul grabbed one final breadstick for the road and had a parting word for Kevin. "Women!," He declared before walking away.

"See you later, Kev," Finn said as he rose to follow Paul.

"Wait a minute." Kevin reached out and grabbed Finn's arm. "I just realized."

"Realized what?"

"I gave her all the money I had on me. I don't have anything for the bill."

"Don't you have a credit card?" Finn asked.

"I did," Kevin replied, "but that's a long story."

"You're incredible," Finn signed as he reached into his pocket and pulled out a wad of bills.

Finn had to break into a half-trot to catch up to Paul. Paul turned to notice Finn at his side. "Sorry I left you, but it looks like it's about to rain any second."

"That's alright," Finn replied.

"Is Ben still in New York?" Paul asked.

"Yeah, I believe he's staying at his mother's house until he gets all her affairs in order."

"Good," Paul nodded. "Call him and tell him we're coming over."

It was one of those typical New York City thunderstorms, intense for a very brief period and very limited geographically. Paul and Finn just made it into the car as the skies opened up, but four miles later as the car parked on Markwood Place, the street was completely dry.

Ben Rothchild was sitting on the porch, slowly rocking in the chair his mother loved.

"Do you gentlemen want to come in?" Ben offered.

"No thanks," Paul replied. "This will just take a minute."

Paul reached into his shirt pocket and remove the four rings. He extended his open hand to Ben. "Here you go. I believe these belong to you."

Ben placed his right hand over his mouth. "Oh my God!" he gasped. "I never thought I would see these rings again. How did you manage to get them from the girl?"

"It was easy," Paul replied. "Actually," he corrected himself, "it was quite bizarre. To prove her innocence the girl flung her handbag at me and demanded that I search it – so I did."

"And the rings were in the bag?" Ben inquired.

"That's right."

"Did you arrest her?" Ben asked.

"If these were normal times," Paul replied. "I would have cuffed her on the spot, but these aren't normal times. I have to deal with ridiculous civilian standard of proof to make an arrest. I have to be 100% sure I have the person who committed the crime or I could end up under arrest for false arrest."

Finn jumped in, "But isn't the fact that she had the rings in her bag enough proof?"

"You're right," Paul said. "If we were just looking to catch a thief – we had her. But we're still looking to catch a murderer, right?"

"I guess so," Finn shrugged. "But how are we going to do that?"

"It's like I said at the restaurant, Finn, there's one more nail to put into that girl's coffin. Then we nail her."

"What's that nail?" Ben asked.

"Like I told Finn earlier, I have a theory about what happened."

"What's the theory?" Ben questioned.

"I think the con artist couple had your mother set up for some big score. Something very big was going to happen on the night she died."

"Big?" Ben exclaimed. "Like what?"

Paul shook his head. "I'm not sure about that, but whatever it was that Agon character was going to do it. I believe the girl left at her normal time and her husband came here a short time later."

"How did he get in?" Ben inquired.

"With a key the girl gave him?"

"I mean how did he get into the community?" Ben clarified.

Paul pointed toward the end of the street. "Right there," he said. "There is a big space between those locked gates that a skinny runt like Agon could easily fit between." Paul paused and took a deep breath. "So, I believe Agon entered the house and was discovered by your mom in the middle of whatever he was trying to do."

"And he killed her," Ben whispered.

"Yes."

Ben's voice returned to a normal tone. "But your theory isn't the final nail in their coffin, is it?"

Paul shook his head. "No, it's not." He pointed across the street. "The Sherman's had CCTV cameras installed after their burglary. I contacted them and it turns out they have a couple of cameras that look out to the front of their house and the street. Those cameras should have seen the girl leave this house at 9PM and then see anyone else who entered and left, including anyone slipping through the gap in the gates."

"Have you reviewed the video yet?" Ben asked.

Paul shook his head. "The Sherman's are away. They'll be back tomorrow morning, so I'll come by and review the video sometime during the afternoon."

"That sounds great," Ben smiled.

"Ok," Paul stretched his arms and yawned. "It's been a long day. I'm gonna head home and hit the hay. I'll call you tomorrow as soon as I review the video."

"Thanks so much, Paul," Ben said. "and have a good night – you too, Finn."

"Goodnight, Ben," Finn waved as he followed Paul down the walkway.

CHAPTER 10: THE TRAP

As Paul made a U-turn on Markwood, Finn probed for the next day's plan of action. "So, do you want me to come with you when you review the video?"

"Video?" Paul laughed. "What video?"

"The Sherman's video."

"There is no video kid. I made all that bullshit up."

"What?"

"That's right, Finn, I never talked to the Sherman's. What do you think, they invite me over for dinner?"

Finn waved to Joey Ryan as Paul's car passed by the booth at Station Square. "I'm totally lost. Where are we going?"

Paul made a right turn onto Austin Street. "You'll see in a minute."

Paul turned onto Union Turnpike and quickly turned off his headlights and pulled to the curb. "Do you know where we are?" Paul asked.

Finn pointed ahead. "Yeah. That's the Markwood gate up ahead."

"Very good," Paul replied. "Have you figured out why we're here?"

"I think so," Finn nodded. "You told Rosa about video at the Sherman's house because you think Agon may try to come get the video before you see it tomorrow."

"You really could have been a detective, kid," Paul chuckled.

The interior light illuminated when Paul cracked the driver's door. "So, now, we're gonna slide through the space between those gates and take up a position of observation in the Sherman's front yard."

"What if he doesn't come?"

"That's a real possibility. For all we know Agon and the girl may be packing their stuff as we speak to make a quick getaway out of New York. If that's the case, some other city will get them – a city that still has a police department."

As they approached the Markwood gates, Paul grabbed Finn's arm. "You have a pistol permit, don't you kid?"

"Yeah," Finn answered, "but my gun is home. I hardly ever carry it."

Paul shrugged. "It's probably just as well."

"What's wrong?" Finn asked.

"It's alright. It's just that I remember how quickly that guy grabbed that baseball bat." Paul slapped Finn's back. "It's ok, I have my gun."

As they approached the iron gates, Paul gently placed his hand on Finn's back to guide him toward the space between the gates. "You go first, kid. This should be no problem for your skinny ass."

Finn turned to the side and extended his arms out to the side. He slid through the gap with only a minimum of effort. Paul attempted to mimic Finn's maneuver, but his girth prevented his passage.

"Grab my hand and pull," Paul directed.

Finn tugged on Paul's right arm, but it was obvious that there was simply too much off Paul to fit through the opening.

Paul attempted to catch his breath outside the gate. "Ok, I'm gonna have to drive back to the main gate, park on the next block and walk up here." Paul pointed to the Sherman's front yard. "Get in behind those large bushes and wait." He began to walk away, but quickly turned around. "Oh, and don't forget to call the main gate and tell the security officer to let me in."

Finn made the call to the Station Square guard booth and then tried to get as comfortable as possible kneeling and sitting behind three large bushes. Although it was very dark on the street, Finn was satisfied with his visibility because the street lights on Union Turnpike backlit the Markwood gates.

The dirt he was sitting in was dry, having been spared the path of the earlier thunderstorm. There was no feel of impending rain from the clouds that failed to blanket the sky. Instead, the cloud cover was sporadic, chaotic in where they chose to be thick or sparse. In the gaps the sky had darkened; the clouds were no longer white or paler grey, instead they were blackened shadows that shifted with the wind. There were times they moved just enough to reveal the full moon, but for the most part Finn realized that this night would be without the benefit of her silvery light.

Finn was becoming anxious. Ten minutes had passed and Paul had yet to appear. His spirits rose when he picked up the distant sound of shoes striking the sidewalk. Finn breathed a huge sigh of relief. That had to be Paul. His relief was short lived, however, when he realized the footsteps were coming from the wrong direction. Paul would be coming from the north on Markwood Place. These sounds were coming from the opposite direction. Finn was perplexed. How was that possible? He couldn't have missed someone sliding through those gates, could he? Finn took a couple of deep breaths. Maybe he was overreacting. Maybe this was simply a community resident out for a nighttime walk. His renewed feeling of calm came to an abrupt end when the footsteps reached such a volume that Finn realized they were on the walkway to the Sherman's front door, directly adjacent to his bushy hiding place.

Finn held his breath and did not move a muscle as a dark figure moved along the path and onto the porch of the Sherman's house. He could make out the figure standing in front of the window to the right of the door.

Finn heard an annoying scratching – squeaking sound coming from the porch. He was uncertain what to do. Should he jump on Agon on the porch, or should he wait for Paul to arrive. But what if Paul never arrived. Finn's internal deliberations ended abruptly when the air was suddenly rent by the sound of breaking glass. No other sound, except for a gunshot could prompt an immediate response, such as Finn bursting out from the bushes and rushing up to the porch.

There were so many dramatic declarations Finn could have made as he approached his prey. He could have used his citizen's arrest power and declared *You're under arrest*!. He might have taken a more tactical approach by shouting, *Get down on the floor*!. He even could have added a dramatic touch with, "*It's all over, dirtbag!* What he did choose was a very subdued, "Hey, don't do that."

The moment before the crowbar struck the right side of his head Finn could see that the dark figure was wearing a ski mask. The blow knocked Finn to the porch floor, and although he never lost consciousness, everything happening around him became a blur. With his head lying against the porch floor Finn perceived voices shouting as well as his head bouncing slightly on the floor as feet stomped and shuffled on the floor.

Though his eyes were open Finn couldn't think of why; his heart was pounding, his mind empty. It was as if a hypodermic of adrenaline had been emptied into his carotid. A nudge to his ribs jerked Finn to a state of semi-awareness – aware enough to recognize Paul's smiling face standing over him.

"Are you alright?" Paul asked.

"I think so," Finn moaned as he ran his right hand along the new welt on his head."

Paul grabbed Finn under the arms. "Let's get you up," he grunted.

Finn grabbed onto the porch fence for support. He needed a moment to orient himself while his world was still spinning. Slowly, the surroundings began to come into focus. His attention was drawn beyond Paul's smiling face to the far end of the porch. Sitting with his hands behind his back and his back against the fence was the dark figure in the ski mask.

Finn kept his grip on the fence and pointed with his other hand. "You got him."

"I sure did," Paul replied. "Unfortunately, I came around the corner just as he was coming upside your head with the crowbar."

Finn rubbed his head again. "Well, at least he didn't get you too."

"For some reason, he had a change of heart," Paul said as he lifted his shirt to reveal his holstered 9mm pistol.

"Hey," Finn gushed, "was Agon alone or is Rosa lurking somewhere around here?"

"I don't know," Paul shrugged. "Let's ask him."

Finn released his grip on the fence and followed Paul over to the seated masked man. Paul turned to Finn. "I think he's had that mask on long enough. Can you take it off him, Finn?"

Finn shuffled forward and grabbed the top of the mask. In one quick motion he pulled it up and off the male's face. Finn stumbled backwards and only a desperate grab for the fence kept him on his feet. His eyes and mouth were open as wide as humanely possible.

"Quite a surprise, isn't it?" Paul remarked.

"I don't believe this!" Finn gasped. "This is not possible."

"No, Finn," Paul replied. "I'm afraid it's very possible."

Finn's wide eyes fixed on Paul. "You knew?"

Paul smiled. "Remember when this started and I told you the story about the woman in the 111th Precinct who was found floating in her bathtub, and how difficult it was to prove a murder by drowning?"

"Yeah, I remember."

"Well, I purposely left out the end of that story."

"What was the ending," Finn asked.

"I told you that there was some truth to the old saying that the butler did it because an investigator should always take a close look at someone who worked in the victim's house."

Finn sighed. "I'm aware of that, Paul. That's why we were looking at Rosa."

"Well," Paul replied, "there's another old saying that says an investigator should always take a close look at the victim's close relatives. In my story about the woman who drowned in her tub, it was her husband who found her. A little research revealed that he had lost his job, had accumulated huge gambling debts, and had recently taken out a large life insurance policy on his wife. It didn't take much to get a full confession."

Finn shook his head and stared at the handcuffed male seated on the porch floor. "I just don't understand, Ben."

Ben Rothchild sat silently, his head hanging down, his eyes fixed on the floor.

Paul shrugged. "All I did was take a look at a close relative and it was all there for me."

"What was there?" Finn questioned.

"Ben got himself involved in some very risky financial investments that didn't work out. He lost a ton of money, but he always thought his mother's money would be there for him one day. But then his mother bought the house and hired the girl and he started having visions of his inheritance disappearing." Paul wagged his finger towards Ben. "But the final straw when his mom took a reverse mortgage on the house."

"Reverse mortgage?" Finn wasn't familiar with the term.

"It's the type of mortgage where a person stops making monthly payments and gets to live in the house for the rest of their life."

"That sounds good," Finn remarked.

"The catch is that the longer the person lives the less equity there is in the house until finally the bank has full equity and when the person dies the bank takes ownership of the home."

"It's not fair." The low trembling voice startled Finn and Paul. Ben Rothchild kept his eyes fixed on the floor. "After my father died I was the one who looked out for her. I was constantly running up here from Virginia to see to her needs. Then, she goes and buys this expensive house without consulting me and takes this ridiculous reverse mortgage. And just to top things off, she hires that girl. All her money would have been gone in less than five years and I would have been left with nothing. It just wasn't fair to me after all I did for her. She lived a long life anyway."

"So, Rosa was completely innocent?" Finn blurted.

"Easy, kid," Paul laughed. "You were right about that girl. Her and her husband are nothing but lowlife con artists – but not murderers."

Finn squinted and pointed at Ben. "So, he was trying to frame Rosa?"

"Not originally. Ben was hoping that his mother's death would be looked on as the tragic case of an elderly woman who had an accident in the tub." Paul glanced at Ben, "And in today's defunded city he probably would have gotten away with it if you didn't latch on to the condition of the shower curtain."

"But what about those rings she had on her tonight." Finn shook his head. "Why would she just hand her bag to you when she knew the rings were inside."

"That shocked me too," Paul admitted. "But when you think about it, it makes sense."

"How?"

"Ben wanted this to look like an accidental death, but if things started going south for him, he wanted a ready-made patsy. The girl probably left her bag in the house on the night of the murder and Ben put the rings in that small compartment inside the bag. Rosa never even realized the rings were in her bag all that time. You saw her reaction when I pulled those rings out of the bag – she was being genuine for once in her life."

Finn scratched his head. "So, why did you go through the charade about the video at the restaurant if you knew Ben did it."

"Hey, Finn, nothing in life is sure. I had a good idea about what happened but I needed to be sure. For all I knew it could have ended up being that slug Agon sitting there in cuffs."

"So, now what happens to Rosa and Agon?"

"Like I said earlier," Paul shrugged. "They are on their way out of New York as we speak. They'll turn up somewhere running their scams."

Finn nodded towards the end of the porch. "And Ben?"

"Well, even in this screwed up city I can still arrest a murderer with this evidence."

"What do we do with him now?"

"I contact the community action liaison to the Queens District Attorney's Office and transport him to the Department of Correction holding facilities in the Queens Courthouse."

"Will he get bail?"

"Who knows?" Paul shrugged. "Anything is possible in this city."

Paul reached down and grabbed Ben under his left arm. "Ok, let's get you out of here."

Finn remained stationery while Paul led Ben down the porch steps. There was one more item to clear up. "Hey, Paul," Finn called. "How did you know the Sherman's were away?"

Paul stopped on the walkway and turned his head. "I didn't. For all I know they're sound asleep upstairs." He began leading his prisoner away but stopped after three steps and turned to Finn again. "I hope you have a good story for them as to how their window was broken."

Finn sighed. "Wonderful."

CHAPTER 11: JUSTICE

June 22nd: Finn stared at his laptop with a degree of surprise. For once, the numbers didn't look that bad. Maybe he wasn't going to sink into the abyss of bankruptcy. He tried to reign in his positive emotions. After all, this was only one day. All it would take was for one more gate to malfunction and his financial situation would return to the brink. Well, at least for the moment the situation was looking up, and he was determined to savor the positive vibe, however fleeting it may be.

Finn's attention was drawn to the burst of light filling the office from the open door. "What's up, Kev?"

"Whew!" Kevin huffed. "I really needed those two days off. I still can't believe I fell for that girl's scam."

"How much did she get from you?"

Kevin stroked his chin. "besides the two hundred from last week, it was twenty dollars here – thirty dollars there. I don't know," he shrugged, "maybe five hundred."

There was a twinkle in Finn's eyes. "I hope you at least got something out of it."

"That's the real tragedy," Kevin exclaimed. "I didn't get anything." He sat at the administrative desk and promptly put his feet up on the desktop. "When am I ever going to learn my lesson with these women?"

"Never," Finn laughed.

Kevin sighed. "You know something, Finbar, you're probably right."

"By the way," Finn inquired. "How's your defense of the lawsuit coming?"

Kevin removed his feet from the desk. "I'm glad you asked." He pointed to Finn's laptop. "Do you get television on that thing?"

"Sure," Finn replied. "I have the Spectrum app."

"Well, put it on," Kevin gushed, "and go to channel 187."

Finn clicked on the Spectrum icon. "What's this all about?"

"Recovering from that girl was not the only thing that tired me out over these last two days. I had to take care of other important business."

"Like what?"

Kevin moved behind Finn to view the computer screen. "What time is it?"

"It's 11AM and here is channel 187. Now what are you talking about?"

Kevin smiled. "Watch."

Finn placed his hand under his chin as he watched the commercial fade to black. The new show was about to begin.

Bongo drums provided the background for the announcer: *This is the plaintiff, Peter O'Malley, the owner of a Queens pub. Mr. O'Malley closed his pub as required by law during the lockdown and traveled to Florida. While he was away, his bartender opened the bar without his knowledge and served food and alcohol to illegal patrons. He is suing the bartender for $2500 for running an illegal speakeasy out of his pub. This is the defendant, Kevin Malone. This bartender contends he was only providing a community service by giving sustenance to those in the community with nowhere else to go. He says it was his good-hearted nature that has gotten him sued. These cases are real. These people are real, here on Judge Jeremy.*

The commercial allowed Finn the chance to properly express his disbelief. "Oh my God! You went on the Judge Jeremy Show!"

"That's right," Kevin crowed. "They taped it the day before yesterday. There was no live audience," he added, "due to the panorama."

"That's pandemic, you moron," Finn growled. "Oh, what's the use."

"Whatever," Kevin replied.

Finn pointed at the screen. "You actually won this case?"

"Hell no," Kevin chuckled. "Judge Jeremy threw me out on my butt."

"So, you still have to pay Pete?"

"I'm not as dumb as you think," Kevin bragged. "My defense was just to get on the show. Both parties automatically get the money in the lawsuit, and since Pete won he gets my share. So, he walks out with five grand and I'm off the hook. It was a win – win for both of us."

"So, do you get your job back?"

"Easy, Finbar," Kevin cautioned. "Let's take one step at a time. I don't have to worry about paying Pete or going to jail. I'll deal with the job issue some other time." Kevin smiled. "Besides, I love working here and you love having me here, right?"

Finn rolled his eyes. "Of course. Who wouldn't want to have you working for them?"

CHAPTER 12: SANITY

December 20th: Finn uncovered his eyes from underneath the covers. He heard the gentle tapping of raindrops against his bedroom window. These were his favorite kind of days where he didn't have to feel bad about not leaving his house early. After all, he was the boss and the boss should be allowed to come in late once in a while. Finn got up and rubbed his knuckles into his eyes. He went downstairs and made himself a hot chocolate with whipped cream and small glittery marshmallows. Finn took his drink into the living room and grabbed a book off the coffee table. He plopped down on the couch underneath the window and watched the rain. Seeing the drops trickle down the window brought a sense of calmness. His upbeat mood was aided by the fact he finally believed he had turned the corner with the business expenses. He had been able to pay his father back the loan he had floated to cover the initial payroll, and he was now actually able to draw his full salary. But it wasn't just his own good fortune that was lifting Finn's spirits.

"Good morning, Finneous," Patrick Delaney sang as he entered the living room with a fresh cup of coffee.

"I know you're feeling great today pop."

"I feel pretty good, Finneous."

"It was a miracle," Finn exclaimed.

"There was nothing miraculous," Patrick replied. "Just rational thinking New Yorkers voting these morons out of office."

"Yeah," Finn cautioned, "but they still had to get a majority in the referendum vote."

Patrick grinned. "After the citizens got to live all these months in a city without police, there was no way that vote was going to go any other way than to bring back the NYPD."

"You're not going back, are you pop?" Finn asked. "After all, you're gonna reach the maximum age soon."

"I'm going back Finneous. I don't want my lasting memory to be crawling away when the department was defunded by lunatics. I want to leave on my own terms."

Finn walked over and gave his father a hug. "I wish you nothing but the best, pop."

...

Finn was surprised when he walked into the public safety office and found the smiling face of George Whitman waiting for him.

"Finn, good to see you," George beamed.

"Good to see you too. What's up George?"

"Let me just say that you've done a great job here with your crew and the community has been thrilled with your performance."

Finn slightly smiled. "That's great to hear, George, but for some reason I sense a 'but' coming."

George forced a chuckle. "You're very perceptive, Finn." He cleared his throat. "The homeowners association held an emergency meeting earlier this morning. Now that the NYPD is back, the community just doesn't see the need for a public safety department."

"So," Finn replied. "You're getting rid of me after this contract period?"

"Not quite," George stammered.

"What then?"

"We're getting rid of you now."

"But we have a contract," Finn snapped.

George's big phony smile remained intact. "Yes, but it clearly states in the contract that the homeowners association reserves the right to terminate the contract at any time – and that's what we're doing at 4PM today." George slapped Finn on the back. "I'm sorry about this, Finn. But you did do a great job."

"Gee, thanks," Finn mumbled as George departed the office.

The door re-opened George's head peeked in. "I almost forgot – Merry Christmas," he grinned.

Finn sat at his desk watching the rain roll down the window. For some reason the news from George had not had a devastating effect on his mood. He still felt pretty good and he wasn't going to force doom and gloom upon himself.

"Hey boss man."

"What's up Sahib?" Finn greeted Biju's appearance in the office.

"I have to talk to you about something," Biju said.

"I have something for you too," Finn responded. "You go first."

Biju looked uncomfortable. "Look, Finn, you helped me and a lot of other people out when we were in trouble. You helped us to keep putting food on our tables and we will forever be grateful to you."

Finn smiled. "This is the second time in fifteen minutes that I feel a 'but' approaching."

"I'm not really sure what you're talking about," Biju said. "But I guess you're right. Me and just about everyone else is going back to the NYPD. You don't know how bad I feel leaving you high and dry."

Finn laughed. "Don't worry about it, Sahib. As of 4PM today you're all fired."

"What?"

"That's right," Finn nodded. "The community doesn't want us now that the police are back."

"Wow!" Biju groaned. "I'm sorry Finn. What are you gonna do?"

Finn put his hands behind his head and his feet up on the desk. "You don't have to worry about me, Sahib. Don't forget, I'm a world famous private eye."

...

December 21st: "Take it easy – slower – lift your end," Finn grunted.

"Easy on the orders," Kevin warned. "You're not my boss anymore. I'm helping you out of the goodness of my heart."

Finn turned at the top of the stairs and slowly backed into his office. "Just a few more feet," he groaned. "Right here is good. Put your end down."

"Finally!" Kevin gasped. "Why the hell did you need this file cabinet anyway? You're back in the private eye business and this cabinet is filled with public safety records."

"What was I supposed to do, leave everything in Forest Hills Gardens? I'm gonna need these records for my taxes." Finn moved behind his old desk and sat in his uncomfortable chair. "Whew, that was heavy," he said as he leaned back and put his feet on his desk. "This old chair is as uncomfortable as ever, but it feels good to be back here." Finn looked out the window to Woodhaven Boulevard. "All I need now is some business."

"Don't worry," Kevin said. "Business will pick up."

"You're right," Finn agreed. "Things are really beginning to open back up. It's the Christmas season and pretty soon husbands and boyfriends will be out cheating again and I'll be back in business. Who wouldn't feel good?" Finn glanced at Kevin. "What about you, Kev? What are you gonna do?"

Kevin smiled. "Don't worry about me, Finbar. The Shamrock is opening tomorrow and guess who Pete called to be his bartender?"

"You're kidding?"

"I guess Pete couldn't get along without the big guy," Kevin bragged.

"I think the five grand Pete got on that court TV show had something to do with his fondness for you," Finn remarked.

"Whatever."

Finn took a deep breath and stretched. "It's kinda weird Kev."

"What's weird."

"Well, just as my business was starting to click I'm dumped. Now I'm back in my shitty private eye office with no business but still I feel good. No," Finn corrected himself, "I feel great."

Kevin took a step back. "I'm not getting too close, Finbar, I think you may have a fever."

"Don't worry about me," Finn assured. "I'm not feverish. As a matter of fact, I just figured out why I feel so good." Finn pointed to the office door. "Because I have her in my life."

"Did I miss something?" Meg asked.

"Not really," Kevin said. "Your boyfriend is just a little feverish."

Finn sprung out from behind his desk. "That's not true. I'm just feeling great because you're here."

Meg gave Finn a hug. "Aw, that's sweet."

"That sickening," Kevin added.

Finn began searching his pockets. "I know they are in here. I'm sure I brought them with me."

"What are you doing, Finn?" Meg asked.

"Something I should have done a long time ago," Finn replied.

Finn pulled his hand out of his pocket. He pulled Meg close and began attaching something on her shirt collar."

"What are you doing?" she asked.

"Just one more second," Finn responded. "There you go, I'm done."

Meg looked down at her collar. "What is this?"

"It's one of the deputy chief stars my dad gave me to wear as public safety director."

"It's very nice," Meg admired, "but why are you giving it to me?"

"Because I don't have a ring yet." Finn answered.

"A ring?"

"That's right babe. I don't want to wait until I have a ring. I want to ask you now."

"Ask me what?"

Finn slowly got down on his good knee. "Marry me!"

"Oh my God!" Kevin groaned. "We have another general."

"Shut up," Finn snapped. "Marry me, babe!"

"Don't do it, honey!"

Finn jerked his head toward the door just in time to see the frail figure of Gladys standing in the doorway.

"You'll be making a huge mistake, dear." Gladys pointed her cane at Kevin. "Just look at the company he keeps. He'll be coming home drunk every night."

"Why don't you keep quiet, you old bat!" Kevin warned.

"You see honey. That's the kind of people your boyfriend associates with."

Finn was still on his knee. He reached up and gently took hold of Meg's chin, guiding her head towards him until their eyes were locked. "Now," he said. "Forget about everyone else here and focus on my question. Will you marry me? What's your answer going to be?"

Meg rubbed the star on her collar then reached forward and ran her hand through Finn's hair. She smiled and took a deep breath. "My answer is...."

About the Author

Robert L. Bryan is a law enforcement and security professional. He served twenty years with the New York City Transit Police and the New York City Police Department, retiring at the rank of Captain. Presently, Mr. Bryan is the Chief Security Officer for a New York State government agency. He has a B.S in criminal justice from St. John's University and an M.S. in security management from John Jay College of Criminal Justice. Additionally, Mr. Bryan is an Adjunct Professor in the Homeland Security Department and the Security Systems and Law Enforcement Technology Department for two New York Metropolitan area colleges. For more information about Mr. Bryan's other books, please visit his website: www.robertbryanauthor.com[1]

---

1.   http://www.robertbryanauthor.com